BO[illegible]

CRIME,

SUSPECT

How a Murder Investigation Really Works

NORAH McCLINTOCK

Illustrations by Paul McCusker

SCHOLASTIC CANADA LTD.

Scholastic Canada Ltd.
175 Hillmount Road, Markham, Ontario, Canada L6C 1Z7

Scholastic Inc.
555 Broadway, New York, NY 10012, USA

Scholastic Australia Pty Limited
PO Box 579, Gosford, NSW 2250, Australia

Scholastic New Zealand Limited
Private Bag 94407, Greenmount, Auckland, New Zealand

Scholastic Ltd.
Villiers House, Clarendon Avenue, Leamington Spa,
Warwickshire CV32 5PR, UK

National Library of Canada Cataloguing in Publication Data

McClintock, Norah
Body, crime, suspect : how a murder investigation really works

ISBN 0-439-98769-5

1. Murder – Investigation – Canada – Juvenile literature. 2. Trials (Murder) – Canada – Juvenile literature. I. Title.

HV8079.H6M33 2001 j363.25'9523'0971 C2001-930335-1

5 4 3 2 1 Printed and Bound in Canada 1 2 3 4 5/0

Contents

Introduction v
1. It Was a Dark and Stormy Night 1
2. The Body 6
3. First Response 10
4. The Investigation Begins 20
5. What the Killer Left Behind 32
6. The Questions Begin 48
7. The Body Reveals Secrets After Death 58
8. The Investigation Continues 65
9. The Crime Lab 82
10. Narrowing the Investigation 95
11. Closing In 109
12. Enter the Lawyers 116
13. The Wheels of Justice Start to Turn 123
14. The Accused's Day in Court 131
15. The Crown's Case 138
16. The Defence Case 152
17. Guilty or Not Guilty? 162
Index 168

To Herman and Sheherazade,
and especially to Spuddie

ACKNOWLEDGMENTS

This book would not have been possible without the help of the people who took time out of their busy days to explain their jobs to me, to answer many, many questions, and to read and offer criticism on what I have written. I want to thank them all.

They are: Valerie Blackmore, Forensic Scientist, Biology Section, Centre of Forensic Sciences; Michael Clarke, QED Forensics; Brian Dixon, Forensic Scientist, Chemistry Section, Centre of Forensic Sciences; Senior Constable Jim Eadie, Forensic Identification, Ontario Provincial Police; Kathy McKague, Forensic Scientist, Toxicology Section, Centre of Forensic Sciences; John McMahon, Director of Crown Operations, Toronto Region, Ministry of the Attorney General; Jean-Paul Menard, Firearms/Toolmark Examiner, Firearms Section, Centre of Forensic Sciences; Patrick Metzler, Metzler Bains Granek, Barristers; Sergeant Lou Morissette, Major Case Management Coordinator, Police Sciences School, Canadian Police College; Dr. Bonita Porter, Chief Deputy Coroner, Inquests, Office of the Chief Coroner; Dr. Toby Rose, Forensic Pathologist, Forensic Pathology Unit, Office of the Chief Coroner; Mark Sandler, Cooper Sandler & West, Barristers and Solicitors; and Detective Anthony Smith, Homicide Squad, Toronto Police Service.

If I have got anything wrong, the fault lies with me, not them.

Introduction

What really happens when someone is found murdered in a big city in Canada?

Who is first on the crime scene?

What steps do police officers take to begin a murder investigation?

How does the investigation proceed?

Who helps police as they try to solve this crime?

How is a suspect finally arrested?

Who prosecutes the crime?

Who defends the accused and what rights does the accused person have?

This book attempts to answer these questions. But every murder case is different. Police officers, forensic scientists, prosecutors and defence lawyers all have their own styles of work. Depending on where in Canada the murder takes place, they may operate slightly differently or have different resources available to them. This book cannot cover all of those differences.

What you will read about are the procedures that are used to investigate and prosecute a typical murder case — if a murder can be called typical.

The case is fiction, but the procedures are real.

Chapter 1

It Was a Dark and Snowy Night . . .

THE SNOW FELL so thickly all day that all you could see was whiteness, as if someone had draped a white velvet curtain around Uncle Joe's cottage. When the sun finally set, the wind came up. It sounded like a million ghosts moaning and sobbing out in the snow-heavy forest. But I wasn't worried. Not until Uncle Joe said, "Uh-oh," and everything went black.

"You okay, Chris?" came Uncle Joe's voice through the darkness.

"Yeah," I said, but my answer sounded like a question.

"You still on the couch?"

I nodded, then realized he couldn't see me. "Yeah," I said again.

"Good. If you get up and walk in a straight line through the kitchen, you'll hit the pantry. On the shelf to the right of the door, there's a box of matches and a package of candles. Think you can find them?"

I said I could.

"Good. I've got a couple of kerosene lanterns in the back room. I'll get them. If you run into any trouble, shout out, okay?"

I said I would, but give me a break — I'd have to come face-to-furry-chest with a ticked-off grizzly bear before I yelled for help. What did he think I was? A scared little kid?

I stood up. It wasn't just dark in the cottage. It was black. Black as the inside of a whale's belly, my dad would have said. Night up here wasn't like night back home, where the streetlights come on before dark and stay on until sunrise. The road into Uncle Joe's place was narrow and winding and covered with dirt when it wasn't covered with snow. There wasn't a single streetlight on it.

It was so dark that I stuck my hands out in front of me so I wouldn't slam into anything on my way to the pantry. I walked in a straight line, just like Uncle Joe said. He must have had the place memorized because he turned out to be dead right. I got through the kitchen without banging into a single table or chair and suddenly there I was in the pantry.

The candles and matches were exactly where he had said they would be. I fumbled a candle out of the box, struck a match and held it to the wick. It flickered, then burned tall. That's when I saw it: a clipping from a newspaper, framed and hung on the wall. I moved in closer with my candle to read it.

Writer shot to death in office

TORONTO — World-renowned children's writer Edwin Scarr was found dead in his downtown office early this morning. He died of gunshot wounds.

Scarr had attended the launch of his newest book last evening at the By the Book flagship store on Bloor Street. More than five hundred young fans lined up to get the author's autograph. Scarr was widely referred to as "Stephen King Jr." because of the popularity of his horror novels, which are aimed

at the adolescent set.

Sources close to the author say that during the book launch, Scarr seemed to be in good spirits, joking with fans and reporters about "the perils of writer's cramp." He left the store at about 9 PM, skipping the reception that followed the book launch. Shortly after midnight, a cleaner found Scarr lying dead on the floor in the downtown office where Scarr wrote and oversaw the mini empire that has grown up around his prolific output. The death has been listed by police as suspicious, and is under investigation.

Funeral arrangements have not yet been announced.

I had read a bunch of Scarr's books and I remembered hearing something about him being killed. But why had my Uncle Joe framed this news story and hung it on his wall?

"Chris? Are you okay?"

"Yeah." I carried the candles and matches back to the living room. As I walked, I saw a weird, wavering light. Uncle Joe had found the kerosene lamps.

Once we could see, he took out his cellphone and made a call. All I could hear was, "Uh-huh. Yes. Oh. I see." Then Uncle Joe put away his phone and said, "The power's out right around the lake. They don't know when it's going to come back on. We'll just have to sit tight."

My stomach fluttered. I didn't know Uncle Joe very well. In fact, I had met him exactly once before, when I was six. I guess that's why Mom had this bright idea. Since my winter break was longer than the time either she or Dad could get off work, she sent me on ahead so I could get to know my uncle. So far all I knew was that he wasn't much of a talker and that he had memorized every inch of his cottage.

I watched him stoke the wood stove. He opened a couple of cans of beef stew and started to warm them on top of the stove. Finally the silence started to get to me.

"So," I said, "what's that clipping all about?"

"What clipping?"

"The one in the pantry."

Uncle Joe frowned. Uh-oh. Had I stumbled onto some deep dark secret? Had my uncle killed Edwin Scarr? Get real, Chris, I told myself. He's a cop, not a murderer. In fact, he was on the Homicide Squad. Hey . . .

"Did you have anything to do with that case, Uncle Joe?"

He nodded.

"Wow! Did you nail the person who did it? Did you have to shoot it out?"

Uncle Joe shook his head. "You watch a lot of TV, Chris?"

I did, but I didn't necessarily want to admit it. Most adults don't think a lot of TV is a good thing.

"Solving a murder isn't exactly like what you see on TV," Uncle Joe said.

I had a good idea of what that probably meant. "You didn't catch him, huh?"

"Did I say that?"

Uncle Joe was a lot like Mom. She never gave you a straight answer, either. She had this idea that you learned more if you figured things out for yourself.

"Give me a break, Uncle Joe. Did you catch the guy or not?"

Uncle Joe stirred the stew.

"You ever seen a dead person before?" he said.

"On TV," I said. "In the movies."

"Lorenzo Rego told me he'd been to a lot of funerals — his grandparents, a couple of old uncles and aunts. But he was pretty shook up the night he punched in the code on the thirteenth floor."

Thirteenth floor? Dead horror writer? Was Uncle Joe pulling my leg? "Who's Lorenzo Rego?" I asked.

Chapter 2
The Body

THE KEROSENE LAMPS filled the room with yellowish light as we dug into bowls of hot stew.

"There aren't as many murders in Canada as there are in some other places," Uncle Joe said. "In 1999, 536 people were murdered in Canada. That's fewer than two murders for every 100,000 people. Sure, it's two too many. But compare that to nearly six murders for every 100,000 people in the United States." The good news, he said, was that three-quarters of Canada's murders get solved.

"But what about Edwin Scarr?" I asked. "And who's Lorenzo Rego?"

• • •

Most people go through life without having anything to do with murder, Uncle Joe said. Lorenzo Rego was one of those people — until a couple of minutes after midnight on April 25, a few years ago.

Rego worked nights as a cleaner in the Belmont Building. By midnight, he should have been on his way home. But when he'd gone up to the thirteenth floor a little earlier, he'd seen lights on in the suite of offices that occupied most of the floor. That meant that the office's main occupant, Edwin Scarr, was working. Rego had instructions never to interrupt Mr. Scarr's work.

Mr. Scarr was a famous writer. Rego had heard that his

books had been translated into more than a dozen languages. Must be nice, he thought. But he couldn't help wondering why people who made it big, like Mr. Scarr, suddenly forgot what life was like for everyone else. Rego had a job to do. It might not seem as important as writing books. But how would Mr. Scarr like it if his office was piled high with garbage, his desk coated with dust and his carpet thick with grime and dirt?

Because it was late and he wanted to go home, Rego checked his watch when the elevator stopped on the thirteenth floor. It was exactly 12:02 AM. As he dragged his cleaning cart out of the elevator, he saw a ribbon of light under the door to Mr. Scarr's office suite. Mr. Scarr must still be inside. Rego hoped that he was getting ready to leave.

He punched in the office security code, opened the door, and pushed his cart inside. It was quiet in the office. He glanced at the cluster of workstations to his right where Mr. Scarr's employees worked. Rego wasn't sure what they all did. He didn't understand why a writer needed so many employees. The area was dark.

Then he looked toward Mr. Scarr's office. The door was ajar. The light was on inside. Pushing his cart ahead of him, he practised what he would say. "Sorry to disturb you, Mr. Scarr, but I was just wondering . . . "

He tapped softly on the door. No answer.

He listened. No sound came from inside. No tippety-tap of Mr. Scarr's fingers on his computer keyboard. No shuffle of his shoes as he paced up and down his "thinking zone" — the part of the office that was not carpeted.

Rego knocked again, louder this time.

Still no answer.

He pushed the door open. At first, he was relieved. The office was empty. Mr. Scarr must have left without shutting off the lights. Or maybe he'd gone down the hall to the men's room. Rego started to push his cart into the office. If Mr. Scarr came back while he was cleaning, Rego would apologize. In the meantime, he could get some work done.

He was halfway through the door when he realized something was wrong. Papers were scattered everywhere. Filing cabinet drawers were open. A wastepaper basket lay on its side. The desk had been swept clear. Papers and pens and pencils lay on the floor.

Then he saw a shoe. A moment later, he realized that there was a foot in the shoe and that the foot was connected to an ankle, which was connected to a leg, which was connected to an entire body.

Mr. Scarr was lying on his back on chocolate-brown carpeting, half hidden by a chair. Rego hurried to his side, crunching papers underfoot. Mr. Scarr was wearing a navy pullover sweater and jacket, which was why Rego didn't spot anything at first. But when he knelt down to check on the unconscious writer, he felt something wet soaking into his pants. He looked closely at the carpet. The area around Mr. Scarr's back was darker than the rest of the carpet. He pressed his finger into the spot. When he pulled it away, it was covered in something sticky and reddish. Blood, he thought. Then he thought, this can't be happening.

Fortunately, the cleaner kept a clear head. He'd taken first-aid training at the factory where he worked during the day. First he checked to see if Mr. Scarr was breathing. He wasn't. Then he pressed his fingers into the side of Mr. Scarr's neck, looking for a pulse. He couldn't find one. He stood up and reached for the phone on the desk. A lot of people would have picked it up and started punching in numbers, but something stopped Rego.

He ran down the hall to Mr. Afton's office, grabbed the phone on his desk and dialed building security. When the security guard didn't pick up on by the third ring, Rego dialed 911. His heart was racing. When the operator answered, Rego forced himself to speak slowly. He gave the address of the Belmont Building. He said that Mr. Scarr was dead. But then as he described to the operator what he had seen, he realized that maybe the writer wasn't dead after all. He said that Mr. Scarr was unconscious in his office, that there was a lot of blood on the carpet and that Mr. Scarr didn't appear to be breathing.

The operator told Rego that an ambulance and the police were on the way. She told him to stay where he was and not to touch anything.

• • •

"Did he turn out to be the killer?" I asked.

Uncle Joe picked up our empty bowls and a kerosene lamp and headed for the kitchen. I followed him with the stew pot.

"Were you one of the cops — "

"Police officers," Uncle Joe said.

Whatever. "Did you end up at the Belmont Building?"

"It's getting late," Uncle Joe said, running water into the sink.

"Aw, please? Just tell me what happened when the cops — police — got there."

Chapter 3

First Response

"On TV, when someone is murdered, things seem to happen fast," Uncle Joe said. "In real life, they do, too. Sort of."

"What do you mean, sort of?" I asked.

"When Lorenzo Rego called 911, an ambulance was dispatched to the scene."

"But Scarr was already dead."

"A person with no medical training saw someone lying in what appeared to be a pool of blood. He said he didn't think that the person was breathing. But maybe he was. Maybe his breathing was shallow."

"He couldn't find a pulse."

"Maybe the pulse was weak, or maybe he looked in the wrong place."

"But the guy was dead!" I said. I had seen the newspaper clipping.

"If you had just been shot, would you want a stranger off the street to assume you were dead, or would you want him to call an ambulance?"

Like I was going to answer that.

• • •

The first priority was to get emergency medical help to the scene and do everything possible to help the victim, Uncle Joe said. Never assume anything.

A patrol car was also dispatched. In murder cases — in

almost any kind of criminal case — patrol officers are usually the first police personnel on the scene.

In this case, Officers Dennis Zelinksi and Stephanie Spinelli hurried to the Belmont. Speed is important when a shooting is reported. The police can't assume that an ambulance will get there first, Uncle Joe said, and the victim may still be alive and need help. If the worst were to happen, the victim might make a dying declaration that could lead to an arrest. And it was always possible that the attacker might still be in the area, although this doesn't happen often.[1] Most crimes are discovered after they have been committed, not while they are in progress. Still . . .

"Never assume anything," I said.

Uncle Joe smiled.

The faster police officers get to the scene of the crime, the more information they can gather. There may be witnesses still at the scene who can provide information. The crime scene itself has to be protected so that evidence isn't altered or destroyed, either by accident or on purpose.

As the two patrol officers approached the Belmont, they watched for anyone who might be fleeing from the area. They heard the *whoop-whoop-whoop* of an ambulance siren. Then, suddenly, the noise stopped. When Officer Zelinski pulled up in front of the building, he saw a security guard locking the main door after ambulance attendants had entered with their equipment and stretcher.

The two officers hurried to the door. The security guard let them in, then re-locked the door behind them. Officer Zelinski asked if the guard knew what had happened.

"It's Mr. Scarr, up on thirteen," the guard said. "He's been shot."

"Who found him?"

"Lorenzo Rego, one of the cleaners."

"Where's he?"

"Still up on thirteen," the security guard said. "They told him to wait there until you guys showed up."

Officer Zelinski made a note of the cleaner's and the security guard's names. He would want to talk to Rego. But first he asked if there were other entrances to the building.

The guard shook his head. There were two emergency exits, one at the rear of the building, one to the east. "But they're exit only," he said. "An alarm goes off when you use them."

"And no alarm went off tonight?"

The guard shook his head.

That meant that as long as the main entrance remained locked and guarded, no one else could enter the building without police knowledge.

Officer Zelinksi asked who else was in the building.

"Apart from Rego, me, and now you guys, I don't think there's anyone here." But the guard didn't sound positive. As soon as back-up arrived, police officers would check the building floor by floor, to see who else was inside and whether they had seen or heard anything.

Officer Zelinksi asked the security guard to take him to the scene of the shooting. Officer Spinelli stayed downstairs to make sure no one entered or left the building.

While they rode up in the elevator, Officer Zelinski asked more questions.

"Did you hear the shooting?"

The security guard shook his head.

"How did you find out what happened?"

"I got a call from Rego. He told me he'd found Mr. Scarr. Told me he'd called 911."

"He called 911 before he called you?"

The security guard nodded.

"When did he call you?"

"A little after midnight."

"Do you know the exact time?"

The security guard's face flushed. "I think it was quarter after," he said.

Officer Zelinski made a note of this. He had already written down the time he and his partner had been dispatched to the scene, the time they had arrived, the exact address of the scene, and the weather conditions outside.

He asked the security guard about the cleaner. What kind of man was he? How long had be been working in the building? Had he had any quarrel with the victim? He asked about the victim, too. What kind of man was he? Did he have any problems? Any enemies? Did the security guard know if he had been in any trouble with the law? The security guard's answers painted Rego as a responsible and reliable worker who got along with everyone. He knew little about the victim, other than that he was a famous writer.

The elevator arrived at the thirteenth floor.

"That's the place," the security guard said, pointing to a door that said Scarr Enterprises. Officer Zelinski headed for it, careful to pass through the open space to one side, not directly in the middle as anyone else might. He knew that the ambulance attendants probably hadn't been as careful. Nor had the cleaner who found the victim. But there was no need to do more damage to the scene.

As Officer Zelinski approached the outer office, the elevator doors opened again and a team of Forensic Identification officers appeared with their equipment. At about the same time, the ambulance attendants came out of an inner office. Their stretcher was empty.

Officer Zelinski took a deep breath. He had been a patrol officer for three years, but had never been involved in a murder before. He thought back to his training and ran through a mental checklist.

The building was secured.

The Ident team had arrived and taken possession of the crime scene. No one would go in or out until they had scoured it for evidence.

He checked with the ambulance crew. They had been in contact with a nearby hospital. The victim had been pronounced dead. The coroner had been called. Officer Zelinski made notes about all of this. He also noted the names of the ambulance attendants, where each one could be reached, where they had moved within the office, what they had touched and whether they had moved the body. He noted the exact time they left.

Then he entered the outer office. A man in cleaner's overalls was standing near the door to an inner office. He appeared dazed. Officer Zelinski tapped him on the shoulder and asked him to step back. The man tore his eyes reluctantly from the body lying on the floor, then obeyed.

Officer Zelinski was going to ask the cleaner how and when he had made his grisly discovery when a detective from the Homicide Squad appeared. Zelinksi briefed her on everything he knew. From here on in, Zelinski's job was to guard the scene. No one would get in without passing him. He would write down the names, addresses and any other relevant information about anyone who entered — including other police officers. He would also record the exact time and date, and the reason they were entering the scene. All of Officer Zelinski's note-taking would be important if and when a suspect was arrested and brought to trial. When that happened, the police could be called to testify. They could be questioned about everyone who entered the crime scene, why they had been allowed to enter, when and for how long they had been there, and what they did when they were there. Nobody knew at this point how long it might take to make an arrest. Unless good records were kept at every step of the investigation, police officers could forget who had done what and why.

• • •

Uncle Joe stretched and yawned. "I don't know about you," he said, "but I'm ready to turn in."

"Aw, come on, Uncle Joe," I protested.

"It's late, Chris."

"But — "

"Maybe tomorrow, okay?"

Maybe?

Officer Zelinski's checklist[2]

First responding officers at a crime scene have many responsibilities. These include:

Take charge of the scene

✓ Make a note of the address, location, time, date, type of call and who is involved.

✓ Be aware of any people or vehicles leaving the crime scene.

✓ Approach the scene cautiously. Be aware of people and vehicles in the area that may be related to the crime.

✓ Make initial observations (look, listen, smell) and ensure officer safety before proceeding.

✓ Remain alert. Assume the crime is ongoing until it is determined to be otherwise.

✓ Treat the entire location as a crime scene until it is determined to be otherwise.

Follow safety procedures

✓ Ensure there is no immediate threat to others (for example, emergency medical personnel). Scan area for sights, sounds and smells that may signal danger.

✓ Approach the scene in a way that will reduce risk of harm to officers and ensure the safety of victims, witnesses and others.

✓ Notify supervisory personnel and call for assistance/back-up.

Attend to emergency care

✓ Check the victim for signs of life and provide immediate medical attention.

✓ If they haven't already been notified, call for medical personnel.

✓ Guide medical personnel to the victim to minimize contamination or alteration of the crime scene.

✓ Point out potential physical evidence to medical personnel. Tell them to have as little contact as possible with this evidence. For example, make sure they leave the clothing and personal effects of the victim as they are. Make sure they don't cut through bullet holes or knife tears. Make a note of anything they move.

✓ Tell medical personnel not to "clean up" the scene or remove anything.

✓ If medical personnel arrived first, get their names, units and telephone numbers.

Control people at the scene

✓ Control all people at the scene. Stop them from altering or destroying physical evidence.

✓ Identify everyone at the scene, including suspects, witnesses, bystanders, victims, victims' family and friends and medical personnel.

✓ Keep unauthorized and non-essential people away from the crime scene.

✓ Make sure no one enters the scene without first putting on a contamination suit.

Identify, establish, protect and secure boundaries

✓ Establish the boundaries of the crime scene, including where the crime occurred, possible points and paths of exit and entry of suspects and witnesses, and places where the victim or evidence may have been moved.

✓ Set up physical barriers (for example, ropes, cones, crime-scene tape or police officers) or use existing boundaries (for example, doors, walls or gates) to keep people away from the scene.

✓ Write down the name of everyone who enters or leaves the scene.

✓ Take steps to preserve and protect evidence that may be lost or damaged (for example, protect the scene from rain, snow, wind — and from footsteps, tire tracks, sprinklers).

✓ Document the original location of the victim and any objects you observe being moved.

Note:

No one should smoke, chew tobacco, use the telephone or bathroom, eat or drink, move any item including weapons (unless this is necessary for the safety and well-being of persons at the scene), adjust the thermostat, open windows or doors, touch anything unnecessarily (note and document any items moved), reposition moved items, litter or spit within the boundaries of the scene.

Hand over control of the crime scene to investigating officer(s)

✓ Provide a detailed crime scene briefing to the investigator(s) in charge.

✓ Help to control the scene.

✓ Remain at the scene until relieved.

Make detailed notes of actions and observations, including:

✓ Observations about the scene, including the location of people and items.

✓ Observations about the appearance and condition of the scene on arrival (for example: lights on or off; shades up or down, open or closed; doors and windows open or closed; smells, ice, liquids; movable furniture; weather; temperature; and personal items).

✓ Personal information from witnesses, victims, suspects and any statements or comments made.

✓ Your own actions and the actions of others.

Chapter 4
The Investigation Begins

I LAY UNDER MY QUILT and tried not to think of ghosts and spirits as I listened to the wind howl. Eventually I closed my eyes. When I opened them again, I was glad to see the sun shining through the window. Things always seem better in the daytime.

It was still snowing, but not as heavily. Uncle Joe's car looked like a big white bump in the driveway. The driveway itself was invisible. I sniffed the air. The smell of coffee made me think of food. My stomach rumbled. I dressed and hurried out of the bedroom.

Uncle Joe was standing over the wood stove stirring something in a pot while he sipped coffee.

"Hungry?" he said when he saw me.

I nodded.

"Good. I'm making oatmeal. We've got enough food to last until the road is cleared and enough wood to keep us warm until the power comes back on."

"How long is that going to be?"

"Probably a day or two for the road," he said. "I'm not sure about the power. It could come on today."

We sat near the stove where it was warm to eat our oatmeal. It was quiet. Too quiet. Uncle Joe didn't seem to mind, but it drove me crazy.

"When did you get to the Belmont Building, Uncle Joe?"

"I was at home, asleep, when I got the call," he said. "The Belmont is a thirty-minute drive from my place. My partner lived right downtown. She got there before me. She was questioning Rego when I got there."

"So he was a suspect," I said. "I knew it!"

• • •

Until you find out differently, Uncle Joe said, you have to treat everyone as a suspect. And Rego was the only witness around. Detective Beth Anthony — Uncle Joe's partner — noticed a dark reddish patch on the right knee of Rego's overalls. She also noticed that he was pale and seemed nervous. Did he have something to hide? Or was he in shock? It was possible that he'd had something to do with Edwin Scarr's death, but Detective Anthony didn't think it was likely. The building had been nearly deserted. It didn't make sense that someone would kill Scarr, call the police and then patiently wait for them to arrive when he could easily have escaped. But stranger things have happened.

Detective Anthony questioned Rego. Her approach was low key. She looked steadily at him and said, "What happened?" That's the most important investigative question a police officer can ask, Uncle Joe said. It gets a person talking, and that's what you want. You want them to tell their story in their own words.

While Rego talked, Detective Anthony took notes. Rego explained how he had discovered Scarr's body. He explained that blood had got on his overalls when he'd knelt down beside Scarr. He told her which phone he had used to call 911. In response to the detective's question, he said that the door to Scarr's suite of offices had been locked when he arrived and that he had let himself in by punching in a code on the security keypad. Detective Anthony made a note to check with the building supervisor to find out who had security codes. She would also ask if it was possible to find out who had used a code to enter the office, and at what time.

Rego said he hadn't seen anyone in the office besides Mr. Scarr.

"Were the lights on, like they are now?" Detective Anthony asked.

They had been on in the reception area and in Mr. Scarr's office, but off in the rest of the suite.

"You said you entered this office a little after midnight. Do you always clean up here at that time?"

Rego explained that he only cleaned late when Mr. Scarr came in late.

That caught Detective Anthony's attention. "What do you mean, when he comes in late? Do you know when he came in tonight?"

"I saw him in the elevator at about quarter to ten," Rego said. "When I got on the elevator on the ninth floor to go up to the tenth, Mr. Scarr was already inside. He was going up. That's when I knew it was going to be a long night."

"Was he alone when you saw him?"

"Yes."

"Did you see anyone else while you were cleaning?"

"No."

"Did you hear anything — a gunshot or anything that sounded like a gunshot?"

"No."

"Were there other cleaners in the building tonight?"

There had been three others. He gave the detective

their names, but didn't know their phone numbers or addresses. His supervisor would know. Then he said, "Poor Mrs. Sloane."

Scarr was the name the writer used on his books. His real name was Edwin Sloane.

Detective Anthony finished questioning Rego. She arranged for him to be taken to the police station to make a full statement. Then she filled in Uncle Joe.

Besides the cleaner, the only other people who had been in Scarr's private office that night were the ambulance crew, the Forensic Identification unit, the coroner — and the killer.

"You didn't go inside even for a minute?" Detective Anthony asked Officer Zelinski. He shook his head. That was a relief. As unbelievable as it sounded, police officers sometimes did stupid things, like walking carelessly into a scene, using the phone, even dropping cigarette butts. It didn't happen often, but when it did, it always caused problems.

• • •

Uncle Joe asked if I wanted more oatmeal. I shook my head.

"This is a murder case, right?" I asked.

He nodded.

"And you were one of the detectives who investigated it, right?"

Another nod.

"So how come when you finally showed up, you stood around talking to the office cleaner instead of looking for clues?"

"Most people think the first thing we do is charge into the crime scene and check it out," Uncle Joe said. "It happens on TV all the time. And I guess it happens in real life in some places, too. Fortunately, it didn't happen in this case."

"Fortunately?"

• • •

When a murder has been committed, the Forensic Identification unit, under the direction of the Homicide Squad, takes charge of the crime scene. They "own" it. They are experts in examining crime scenes and collecting evidence. Generally, they keep everyone out until after their job is done.

Another person — the coroner — "owns" the body. The coroner decides when the body can be removed from the scene and orders the postmortem examination or autopsy, which is done by a pathologist.

By law, a coroner must be notified whenever there is an unnatural or unexplained death. This includes cases in which foul play, suicide, accident or negligence is suspected. Sometimes coroners investigate deaths from natural causes.

The coroner's job is to answer five questions. *Who is the deceased person? Where did the person die?* This isn't always clear. Sometimes bodies are not found in the place where the death occurred. *When did the person die?* In a murder case, time of death can eliminate suspects, break alibis and help convict murderers. *How did the person die?* — in other words, what was the medical cause of death? And, finally, *What was the manner of death?* There are five possible answers to the last question: natural causes, accident, suicide, homicide and undetermined.

Dr. Susan Carlisle from the coroner's office arrived

shortly after the Ident team and examined Edwin Scarr's body. She told the detectives that he had been shot twice in the chest. From the location of the wounds, she didn't think it was suicide. All indications were that he had died where he had been found — in his office.

Examination of the body can provide some idea of when death occurred. Body temperature can give a clue, but it can be affected by many factors, such as how much clothing the person was wearing, the temperature of the environment in which the person was found, and whether the person was in a struggle before death. Another clue is given by the rate at which the body stiffens after death. The stiffening is called rigor mortis. The coroner's office uses a general guideline: if the body is warm to the touch and there is no rigor, death probably occurred within four hours. If the body is warm to the touch and rigor has started, death probably occurred within four to eight hours. If the body is cold to the touch and rigor is present, then the person has probably been dead for more than eight hours.

Another clue to time of death is postmortem lividity. After death, the heart stops pumping. Blood stops flowing. It settles in the lowest points of the body. If a person is lying on his back when he dies, the blood settles on the back of the body. This starts about thirty minutes after death. After eight to ten hours, the blood stays where it has settled and will not move. This can also give a good idea of the position of the body at the time of death. In Edwin Scarr's case, lividity had started.

But estimating time of death by examining a body is an inexact science. Usually, the best time-of-death estimates come from witnesses who can tell the police when the victim was last seen alive. Rego had seen Edwin Scarr arrive at his office at 9:45 PM. He had discovered Scarr's body a few minutes past midnight. This meant that Scarr had died some time between 9:45 and midnight. The coroner wouldn't be able to pinpoint the time of death any more accurately than that.

People often think that a body is taken to the morgue as soon as it is found. In some cases, this is true. A body may be moved quickly to protect evidence. Wind, rain and snow can damage evidence on a body found outdoors.

But in this case, there was no hurry. The body would stay where it was until the crime scene had been thoroughly documented and measurements made so that the body could be accurately located in the crime-scene sketches that would be prepared.

Uncle Joe and Detective Anthony stayed out of the way and let the Ident officers do their job. One thing the Ident officer told them right away was that the office had been ransacked. That raised a couple of questions: Had the victim walked in on a robbery? If so, what had been stolen?

While they waited for more information, the detectives got someone to locate Scarr's office manager. Then they went to talk to the security guard.

Uncle Joe had noticed a security camera in the building lobby.

"Does that thing work?" he asked. The security guard shook his head. Uncle Joe tried to hide his frustration. If the camera had been working, it could have told him who had been in and out of the Belmont that night.

"Is there any other record of who's been in here tonight?" he asked.

The security guard showed the detectives a visitors log, in a loose-leaf binder. Only two visitors had signed into the building after it had closed — one was a 6:30 PM pizza delivery to an ad agency on the tenth floor, the other an 8 PM courier delivery to a design company on the fourth floor.

"A courier at 8 PM?" Detective Anthony frowned. That didn't sound right.

"Design companies always seem to have weird deadlines," the guard said.

The detectives would check out both deliveries.

"When did the victim arrive?" Uncle Joe asked.

"He could have come in any time," the security guard said. He explained that people who worked in the building didn't have to log in. They had security codes and could let themselves in even when the security guard was on his rounds.

"We're going to need a list of all the tenants," Uncle Joe said.

By the time they went back upstairs, the Ident officer in charge had more information for them.

"We spotted a cartridge case," he said.

That could mean that a semi-automatic weapon had been used. By studying the cartridge case — the outer shell of a round of ammunition — a firearms examiner could possibly tell what kind of gun had been used.

"Just one?" Detective Anthony asked. The coroner had said that the victim had been shot twice. If both shots had come from the same gun, there should be a second cartridge case.

"Just one so far," the Ident officer said.

"Murder weapon?"

"Not that we've been able to locate."

"Anything else?"

"It looks like the victim was at a book launch earlier this evening." He showed the detectives a printed invitation, now sealed in plastic, for the launch of Edwin Scarr's latest book. The launch had been scheduled from 6 to 8:30 PM, with a reception immediately following. It had been held at a large bookstore downtown.

A uniformed officer beckoned to the detectives.

"We've located the victim's secretary," he said.

• • •

"Is she important to the case?" I asked. "It turns out she was madly in love with Scarr and he didn't feel the same way, so she killed him, right?"

"You'd better get your boots on," Uncle Joe said.

"Why?"

"We're low on firewood. We have to bring some in from the shed."

"But I want to know what happened next."

"First wood. Then talk," Uncle Joe said.

Coroners and Medical Examiners[3]

The first coroners took up their duties as early as 1194 in England, when Richard the Lionheart was king and Robin Hood made his home in Sherwood Forest. A document called the "Articles of Eyre" directed each county to elect "keepers of the pleas of the Crown." This was eventually shortened to "crowner" or "coroner."

Coroners in the Middle Ages had many duties,

including holding public inquiries — inquests — into unexplained deaths. These included homicides and suicides. At that time, death investigation had more to do with putting money into royal coffers than with making sure that justice was done. A person convicted of murder forfeited his property to the Crown. The coroner was responsible for holding the accused's property until after the trial.

By the 1700s, coroners focused solely on death investigation. When a coroner was notified of a sudden or unexplained death, he ordered a constable to gather a minimum of twelve jurors. The jury viewed the body with the coroner and considered whether the death was accident, suicide or murder. They also considered what had caused the death. For example, was the person stabbed? If so, with what? The jurors examined any wounds that may have caused the death.

In Canada, each province has its own system for investigating untimely, suspicious and preventable deaths. A coroner system is used in New Brunswick, Quebec, Ontario, Saskatchewan, British Columbia, Northwest Territories, Yukon and Nunavut. In Ontario, coroners must be medical doctors in good standing. In British Columbia, coroners don't need any special training or expertise. Prince Edward Island, Nova Scotia, Manitoba and Alberta use a medical examiner system. Medical examiners are usually medically trained professionals. Newfoundland abolished its coroner system in 1875. In that province, provincial court judges hold inquiries into sudden or unexplained deaths.

STANDING BACK AND OBSERVING THE CRIME SCENE[4]

Police officers involved in homicide investigations have to be alert and observant. Small details can provide important information about what happened, who was involved, what the motive might have been and who may have seen something useful. When arriving at a murder scene, police officers look for — and make notes on — the following things.

Doors: How many? Where do they lead? Are they locked or bolted? From inside or outside? Are there any signs of forced entry? Scratches or pry marks?

Windows: How many? Are they open or closed? Are there window coverings, such as blinds or curtains? Are they up or down? What is directly across from the windows?

Papers or mail on desk: What kind of papers or documents are they? Is mail opened or unopened?

Lighting: Were lights on when death was discovered? How are the lights controlled? Where are the switches?

Smells: Is there any smell of perfume, alcohol, tobacco, gun powder?

Heating conditions: What is the temperature? Is the heating or air conditioning on?

Signs of visitors: Are there any bottles, cups or glasses at the scene? If so, how many? What is in them? Are there any lipstick marks on them? Other marks?

Contents of ashtrays and wastepaper baskets

General disorder: Is there evidence of a struggle? Is the area dirty or disarrayed?

Shooting: How many bullets were fired? Are they all accounted for? Cartridge cases (number and location)? Bullet holes (number and location)?

Blood: Where is it located? What is the degree of coagulation? What is the size and shape of the bloodstain or pool of blood?

Stairs, passages, entries and exits: Check for footprints, debris and discarded items to determine route used by suspect.

Presence of items that do not belong: For example, a ski mask in a business office.

Absence of items that should be there: For example, the victim's wallet or vehicle.

CHAPTER 5

What the Killer Left Behind

THE SHED BEHIND Uncle Joe's cottage was piled high with firewood, so we wouldn't freeze while we waited for the power to come on. But we had to wade through thigh-high snow to get to it. Even though Uncle Joe slogged through the yard ahead of me, making a trail, it was hard going. I was sweating by the time I got to the shed. Uncle Joe piled firewood into my arms, and then stocked up himself. We made four trips in all. By the time we had finished, the top half of me was dripping with sweat and the bottom half was frozen almost solid.

"Get changed," Uncle Joe said. "I'll make us some cocoa."

Uncle Joe's cocoa was the best I had ever tasted. My teeth stopped chattering as I sipped it.

"So, how do you like my big murder case so far?" Uncle Joe asked.

"That depends," I said. "What happened next?"

Uncle Joe's blue eyes twinkled. "The really exciting stuff. The stuff they never show you on TV."

"You mean, you arrested the perp and gave him the third degree until he confessed?"

"Very funny," Uncle Joe said. "No, what happened was that the Ident guys got to work."

• • •

Anyone who thinks that police work is jam-packed with

glamour and excitement hasn't spent a lot of time with Forensic Identification officers, Uncle Joe said. These officers sometimes seem as exciting as accountants or librarians. They're a-place-for-everything-and-everything-in-its-place kind of people. They can spend hours, even days, picking through a crime scene looking for evidence. They record every piece of evidence they find and everything they do to it. It's slow, careful work — like cutting a couple of acres of grass with a pair of nail scissors. If Forensic Identification officers do their work well, they can clinch a case. If they mess up, the result can be one more bad guy on the streets.

Officer Durning was the Identification officer in charge of the Scarr crime scene. He was a methodical man who worked according to a theory developed in 1920 by French criminologist Edmond Locard. Locard's theory was that every contact leaves a trace. Every time one object comes into contact with another object, it takes something from that object or leaves something behind. Think of cat hairs clinging to your pants. Or the marks your fingers leave on a clean glass. Or the impressions your boots make when you walk in snow or on damp ground.

Officer Durning believed that physical evidence is the most powerful type of evidence. Unlike eyewitness identifications and witness statements, physical evidence is unaffected by emotion, prejudice or personal impressions. If it's carefully collected, properly stored and well documented, physical evidence never forgets. It doesn't take sides. And it doesn't lie.

Officer Durning also believed that crime scenes are non-renewable resources. No one can enter a crime scene without running the risk of changing something, moving something, damaging something, leaving something behind or taking something away. Officer Durning and his team had only one chance to get things right.

When Officer Durning arrived at the Belmont Building in the early hours of April 25, the first thing he did was pull on a "bunny suit." This special contamination suit went over his clothes and covered his head. It would keep him from dropping any hairs or fibres, which could contaminate the scene. He pulled "booties" on over his shoes and gloves onto his hands. Everyone who got off the elevator on the thirteenth floor had to do the same thing.

Next he asked the police officer in charge of securing the crime scene about the actions of everyone who had entered it. He made notes about what he was told. He wanted to be clear about what he was looking at when he finally examined the scene.

When Officer Zelinski told him that the body had been found by an office cleaner, Officer Durning held his breath.

"Please tell me he didn't clean up," he said. It sounds silly, but Ident officers have arrived at crime scenes to discover that the owner of the house or building has "tidied up." Usually this isn't a deliberate attempt to destroy evidence. Often it's a reaction to stress. People are upset after discovering a serious crime. Some clean up to keep busy. Some do it by reflex — you're supposed to tidy up when visitors, even police officers, are expected. It wouldn't have surprised Officer Durning to learn that Rego had vacuumed or dusted while he waited for the police.

Next, Officer Durning asked the cleaner about his actions inside the office. Where had he walked? What had he touched? He asked to see the bottoms of Rego's shoes. The cleaner looked surprised. Officer Durning explained that seeing the shoes would help him understand any footwear impressions he might find inside the office. The cleaner still looked confused.

"Footprints," Officer Durning explained.

Rego nodded. Officer Durning peered closely at the underside of the cleaner's shoes. He looked at the dark stain on the knee of the cleaner's overalls.

"Would you mind if we borrowed your shoes for a while?" he said.

The cleaner looked alarmed. "I didn't do anything," he said.

Officer Durning understood his worry. Nobody likes to be under police scrutiny. He explained that there appeared to be blood on the bottom of the left shoe. If it had tracked any blood on the floor or carpet in the office, Officer Durning wanted to know. If the killer's shoes had also have left traces of blood, Durning needed to know whose shoes were whose.

Rego agreed.

Next, Officer Durning checked the layout of the entire office suite. He had been told that the only areas anyone had entered that night were the victim's office, the corridor leading to the front door of the suite and the corridor leading to the office where the cleaner had called 911. Officer Durning headed there first to check if the cleaner's shoe had tracked any blood down the hall. He saw a transfer strain on the grey carpet. A transfer stain is made when a substance, such as blood, is transferred from one object to another. In this case, it was transferred from the bottom of Rego's shoe to the carpet. He also noticed two drops of blood just outside the office door. He marked both areas, then went back to the victim's office. He did not enter the office. Instead, he stood at the door and looked inside.

Scarr's office was large and square. The floor was littered with papers. To one side of the office, near the windows, was a large L-shaped desk. A computer sat on the shorter

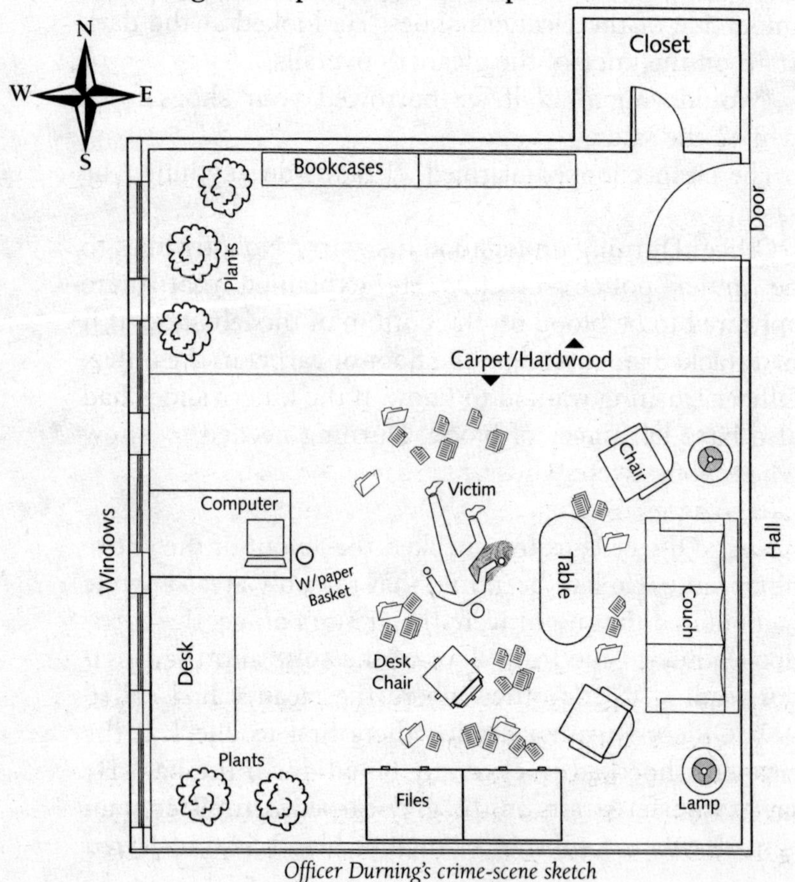

Officer Durning's crime-scene sketch

arm of the L. The screen was blank. There were no shining lights to show that either the monitor or the CPU was switched on.

The windows beside the desk ran from about a metre above the floor all the way to the ceiling. The mini-blinds covering them were open. A black leather swivel chair sat in the middle of the room, near the body. There was a black leather couch along one wall. Immediately in front of it was a low, brass-legged table with a glass top piled with papers. Two wooden filing cabinets with brass handles stood along another wall. Two of the file drawers were partly open and three were open almost the whole way. From the haphazard look of the contents, Officer Durning guessed that most of the files now lay on the floor.

He noticed an overturned wastepaper basket. Nearby were some orange peels and some crumpled foil that looked like the wrapping from a chocolate bar. The wall above the filing cabinets was hung with framed photographs and certificates. Officer Durning squinted at them from the doorway. They looked like awards of some kind. A fourth wall was filled with floor-to-ceiling built-in bookcases crammed with books. The shelves did not appear to have been disturbed.

Two-thirds of the office floor was covered with thick, dark-brown carpet. The rest was highly polished hardwood. There was track lighting overhead and it was on. Both the cleaner and Officer Zelinski had said the lights were on when the body was found.

Finally, sprawled on the carpet, face up, was the victim. He looked to be in his forties. He was dressed in a pair of grey slacks, a navy pullover sweater and a navy jacket.

His black loafers were well polished. Durning saw what he assumed was blood on the carpet near the body.

Officer Durning was in no rush as he studied the office. His first step before entering any crime scene was to look and think. He knew that the office contained evidence that was just waiting to be collected. As long as no one did anything dumb, that evidence wouldn't move.

Three stages of work faced him and his team.

The first was a "non-invasive" examination of the scene. This meant studying the scene without touching or disturbing anything. Were there any obvious objects lying on the floor? A gun? Cartridge cases from a fired bullet? Matches or cigarette butts? Cups or glasses that might have fingerprints on them? Had anything been broken, perhaps during a struggle? Were bloodstains visible? What about footprints that could have been made by shoes or boots worn by the killer? An officer can often detect footprints on a hardwood floor or other smooth flooring by darkening the room, holding a flashlight about an inch above the floor and shining it over the floor at an angle. The same technique can also be used to find the tiny pieces of evidence — hairs and fibres, for example — that are known as trace evidence.

Officer Durning bent to look under the desk to check if the power bar was switched on or off. He was surprised to see that it was on, but that one of the cords lay unplugged beside it. He followed the cord back to the CPU. It looked like someone had unplugged the computer. Why would anyone do that instead of switching off the power bar?

Officer Durning saw, but did not touch, one cartridge case lying on the carpet under the desk. The coroner had said that the victim had been shot twice, but Officer

Durning didn't see a second cartridge case. Maybe it was hidden under the litter. If it was, that could mean that the victim had been shot before the office was trashed. That would suggest that the victim hadn't been killed because he'd stumbled onto a robbery in progress.

After Officer Durning had noted the visible evidence, but before he touched or moved anything, he began to document the crime scene — to make a visual record that would show exactly where everything was when the body was discovered. He did this in two ways.

First he videotaped the scene, starting with a general overview, then focusing in on details. He was careful to move the video camera slowly. At this point, he wasn't sure what might turn out to be important. He didn't want to speed over anything that might later turn out to be critical to the case. After he finished taping, he labelled the videocassette. He also wrote down the date and time he had shot the videotape, and how long it ran. Like all good Ident officers, he made notes about everything.

He would give the videotape to the two homicide detectives so that they could study the crime scene without running the risk of contaminating it. They could view everything at their leisure, which would let Officer Durning take his time processing the scene.

Next he set up a camera and tripod and took crime-scene photographs. Photos make a better-quality image than videotape does. They can be blown up to show more detail.

Officer Durning took a series of photos to show the overall layout of the scene. He took photos from the four corners of the office. Then he photographed each piece of evidence he had found: the body, the bloodstains, the cartridge case, the footprints on the hardwood floor. He took these pictures from a medium range so that anyone looking at them could see where each item was in relation to everything else in the office. Finally, he took several close-up pictures of each piece of evidence. The first showed the item just as it was. Then he placed a small ruler next to the item and took a second picture to show exactly how big the item was. He included a direction marker in each photo to show North. He made notes about the photos he was taking and what each would show.

It was a lot of work, but he knew from experience that when a case got to court, anything could be questioned. For example, he had to be able to say for sure that he had found a cartridge case lying in a specific place pointing in a specific direction. If he couldn't — or if he seemed unsure about the details of one piece of evidence, the defence could use that to cast doubt on other evidence he had collected.

After he had finished taking photographs, he moved on to another task — collecting all visible evidence.

This had to be done carefully so that nothing would be damaged. For example, wet or damp items would be packaged in paper and dried before being submitted to the lab. Moisture allows micro-organisms to grow, and these can destroy or alter evidence. Items are usually packaged separately. The cartridge case that Officer Durning had spotted would be sealed in a small cardboard box. If he later found the second case, it would be packed in its own box.

He collected samples of blood from the large stain on the carpet. These would be analyzed for DNA, which would tell the detectives whether all the blood came from the victim, or whether blood from someone else was present. Knowing whether or not the killer was wounded could be helpful.

Most crime scenes contain hairs and fibres that can be important in proving that a suspect was there. When most people think of fibres, they imagine pieces of thread. But often the fibres collected at a crime scene are tiny and not clearly visible to the naked eye. There may be millions of them. They have to be painstakingly collected.

Officer Durning did this a few inches at a time. He peeled off some clear adhesive tape and patted the surface of each item — the carpet, the couch cushions. He transferred the tape, and the fibres clinging to it, to a white backing and labelled it. Then he peeled off another piece of tape. Depending on the scene, taping could take hours.

Each piece of evidence was packaged, sealed, labelled and logged. At each stage of a homicide investigation, all of the evidence had to be accounted for. The police did not want to be accused of sloppiness or of allowing anyone to tamper with the evidence.

After the obvious pieces of evidence had been collected, Officer Durning moved to the next stage of his search. He wouldn't yet rearrange anything in the crime scene, but he would introduce new elements — things like powders to "lift" fingerprints and footprints, and spray-on chemicals.

He and his team dusted for prints on the desk, the filing cabinet drawers, the computer and the computer screen. He inspected the computer plug that had been pulled from the power bar and saw blood on it. The cord would have to be removed from the computer and the blood checked.

After he had dusted each item, Officer Durning took close-up photos of each fingerprint. He also took shots that showed where each print was in relation to the crime scene. He made more notes. Then he "lifted" the prints and fixed them to white backing for future analysis.

Fingerprints are important evidence because every individual's prints are unique. Even identical twins have different fingerprints. Criminals often wear gloves so they won't leave fingerprints behind. They wipe their finger-

Taping lifted fibres to a backing

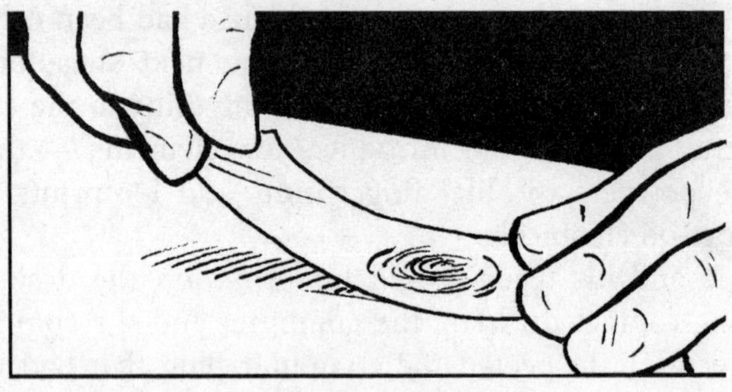

Lifting fingerprints

prints off weapons like guns and knives.

But even though every criminal has to enter and leave the crime scene, they seldom think about footprints and don't try to hide their footwear. Because of this, they often leave behind footprints or footwear impressions. Footprints sit on the surface of a floor or other hard surface. They're made when a shoe leaves behind dust, water, mud or other substances. Footwear impressions are made when a shoe or boot sinks, even just a little, into a surface like snow or damp ground.

Each type of footwear has its own characteristics. The tread of one brand of popular sneaker is different from the tread of a rival brand. These treads can often be used to identify the type of footwear a criminal was wearing. And no two pairs of shoes or boots wear in the same way. Over time, people put their own marks on treads, depending on the surfaces they walk on, the way they walk, whether or not they run, and so on. It's often possible to link a specific pair of shoes to a crime scene.

Officer Durning collected footprints in the room in much the same way he collected fingerprints. He dusted them with fingerprint powder and lifted them with wide strips of fingerprint tape.

By the time he finished, hours had passed. Scarr's body had been transported to the morgue long before the Ident team began the final stage of its search — taking apart the crime scene to look for hidden evidence. Officer Durning particularly wanted to find the missing cartridge case and any bullets.

Cartridge cases could end up in strange places. Officer Durning had found them in flowerpots and caught in the tops of curtains. Bullets could be easier or harder to find than cartridge cases. They were easier to find if they struck a wall or piece of furniture, leaving a hole. They were harder to find outdoors. In particularly tough cases, an explosives dog would be called in. These specially trained animals can sniff out bullets and cartridge cases — even those that are buried or covered with snow.

Officer Durning had spotted some splintering and a hole in one of the filing cabinets. He looked closely at it now and saw that something was embedded in it. A bullet. He used a small saw to cut around the bullet. Prying it out would damage it.

When Identification officers start to move things, they have to be careful not to accidentally destroy any hidden evidence. Again Officer Durning stood back and made a plan. He had already photographed the partially bloody footprints that he had seen on some of the papers littering the office. Now would come a more difficult task. The good news was that whatever lay beneath the mess of papers had probably been protected from any damage done by the cleaner and the ambulance attendants. The bad news was that the papers would have to be examined one by one before being taken away to a safe place. This would take time.

Officer Durning worked patiently until he got a call asking him to attend the autopsy. He left his team in charge of continuing the work and keeping the scene secure.

• • •

"I can see why you're not an Identification officer," I said to Uncle Joe.

"What do you mean?"

I glanced around the cottage. It wasn't dirty, but it wasn't exactly what you'd call tidy, either.

"I bet Officer Durning's CD collection is alphabetized," I said. "I bet the socks in his sock drawer are in neat rows, sorted by colour. I bet — "

"I get the picture," Uncle Joe said. "And, yes, he's well organized. And what he does is critical. I remember a robbery case a few years ago. By the time Durning had finished with the scene, he knew how the thief had got in, exactly where he had been once he was inside and which way he went when he left. He even knew the colour of the gloves the guy had worn. The suspect confessed. He thought he'd been caught on a security camera. Guys like Durning are trained to see and interpret things that most people don't notice."

"So far it sounds like he was doing all the work," I said. "Where were you and your partner while he was at the scene? Back home in bed?"

"I wish," Uncle Joe said.

Outfitting a Crime Scene Identification Officer[5]

Forensic Identification officers need a lot of equipment to get the job done. Here are just a few of the items in their bag of tricks.

Fingerprint equipment, including brushes, powders (black and silver), tape, lift cards and a magnifying glass.

Casting equipment (for making moulds), including plaster of Paris, dental powder, silicone casting material, mixing bowls, rubber spatulas, reinforcement mesh, plastic bags, wooden tongue depressors, modelling clay, identification tags with string, and snow wax (for taking impressions in snow).

Photography equipment, including cameras, lenses (normal, wide angle, macro and telephoto), film (colour and black & white), flash attachments, batteries, tripod with adjustable head and legs, measuring devices and disposable rulers, filters, lens brush and lens tissue, camera carrying cases and shutter release cable.

Evidence packaging supplies, including paper bags, paper, cans, vials, evidence tape, marking pen, stapler and pill boxes.

Blood collection supplies, including sterilized cloth squares, sterilized thread, glass microscope plates, distilled water, scalpel and disposable scalpel blades, tweezers and small scissors.

Deceased print kit (for fingerprinting the victim), including rollers, black ink, finger strips, plain paper and ink remover.

Hand tools, including claw hammer, hacksaw, screwdrivers, pliers, pipe wrench, pry bar, vise grips, wire cutters, bolt cutters, socket set (metric and standard), wood chisels, hand axe, shovels, sifters, automobile door-handle remover, measuring tapes and pocket knife.

Biohazard kit, including disposable latex gloves, footwear protectors (booties), face mask/shield, gown/apron and biohazardous waste bag.

Miscellaneous equipment, including flashlight and spare batteries, paper and report forms, graph paper for scale drawings, clipboard, pens, chalk and crayons, cellophane tape and dispenser, clear book-binding tape, extra evidence tape, staples and stapler, scissors, scalpels and replacement blades, large and small forceps, compass, large magnet, nylon rope, electrical cord and metal detector.

CHAPTER 6

The Questions Begin

"WHAT DO YOU MEAN, you wish you'd been back in bed?" I asked. "What happened? Did you corner the suspect? Did he shoot at you, Uncle Joe? Did he hit you?"

"Worse," Uncle Joe said.

The only thing I could think of that was worse than being hit was being killed, and Uncle Joe looked one hundred percent alive to me.

"I've been a police officer for sixteen years and on the Homicide Squad for eight years," Uncle Joe said. "You'd think I'd get used to it."

"Get used to what?"

"Breaking the news."

• • •

Edwin Scarr's secretary was waiting in the security office on the first floor of the Belmont Building. Martha Cooper was a motherly looking woman. She looked worried when she saw the detectives.

"They told me something happened, but they didn't tell me what," she said, "and they wouldn't let me go upstairs. Was it a robbery?"

The detectives introduced themselves. As soon as Uncle Joe said the word "homicide," Martha Cooper's face went pale.

"What's happened?" she said. "You're not going to tell

me that someone was . . . " Her voice trailed off.

"I understand you're Mr. Scarr's secretary," Uncle Joe said.

"That's right."

"I'm sorry to have to tell you that Mr. Scarr has been shot. I'm afraid he's dead."

"Who did it? Who killed Mr. Scarr?" Martha Cooper asked.

"We were hoping you might have some ideas about that."

The secretary shook her head. "Everyone liked Mr. Scarr," she said. "He could be demanding at times, but he was a good man. Children adored him."

"I understand he was quite well known," Uncle Joe said.

"Quite well known?" the secretary echoed. "That's like saying Stephen King is quite well known. Mr. Scarr sold millions of books in dozens of countries. I can't imagine who might have wanted to hurt him, let alone kill him."

"You mentioned robbery," Detective Anthony said. "Is there any special reason for that?"

There was a men's shelter a few blocks from the Belmont, the secretary said, and homeless men often hung out in a nearby park. But she had to admit she had never heard of a robbery in the building.

"Did Mr. Scarr keep valuables in his office?" Detective Anthony asked.

"Only whatever manuscript he was working on"

The detectives asked more questions. Did Mr. Scarr have any unhappy employees? Had he received any threats? Had he ever been involved in anything that might have involved him with a bad crowd? To each question, Mrs. Cooper answered no. They asked about Mr. Scarr's next of kin and learned that the late author lived with his second wife. The couple had been married for less than two years. Martha Cooper gave them the address and offered to call Scarr's widow.

"Thank you, but we'd rather talk to her in person," Uncle Joe said, adding, "At some point we'll need you to tell us if anything is missing from his office."

Martha Cooper seemed happy to be able to help in some way.

The detectives set out for Edwin Scarr's house, which turned out to be a mansion surrounded by a black iron fence in one of the city's best neighbourhoods. By the time the detectives passed through the gate, it was nearly three o'clock in the morning. Despite the late hour, the porch light was still on. Lights were also on in the front hall and in several other windows.

The detectives climbed the sturdy stone steps to the front door and rang the doorbell. A few seconds later, a woman's face appeared in the small window set into the thick door. She peered at them with worried eyes. Who wouldn't be troubled to see two strangers on their porch in the middle of the night? She opened the door, but left the security chain in place.

"Mrs. Jennifer Sloane?" Detective Anthony said. They had learned her name from Scarr's secretary.

When the woman nodded, the detectives introduced themselves and showed their identification.

"We'd like to talk to you about your husband," Detective Anthony said.

Mrs. Sloane looked even more apprehensive. She unhooked the security chain and opened the door.

"What's happened?" she said.

The detectives had delivered terrible news more times than they cared to think about. There was no easy way to do it. Detective Anthony explained what had happened.

Mrs. Sloane stared at her for a moment, stunned.

"But how? Who — ?"

"We'd like to ask you some questions, Mrs. Sloane, so that we can try to understand exactly what happened."

Mrs. Sloane opened the door and showed them into the living room. Both detectives automatically studied the woman's expression to see if it seemed genuine. It sounds awful, Uncle Joe said, but when you deliver the news to a grieving relative, you have to remember that you could be talking to the killer. In most cases, the victim and the killer know each other and, at this point in their investigation, the detectives had only a few basic facts about Edwin Scarr. They knew less about his wife. They knew nothing at all about the couple's personal life. They had to keep in mind that Mrs. Sloane might have had a reason to want her husband out of the way.

"Was there any special reason your husband was working late tonight?" Detective Anthony asked.

The widow shook her head. "He often went to the office for a few hours at night."

"Do you have any idea what time he might have arrived there?"

"He went there right from the book launch." In a shaky voice, Mrs. Sloane told them about the event that had taken place earlier that evening. "The place was filled with children. They all wanted his autograph."

"Were you at the book launch, Mrs. Sloane?"

"Yes."

Patiently, the two detectives gathered details about the event: who had organized it, how long it had lasted and who had been there. It wasn't easy to have to ask a family member so many questions, Uncle Joe said. Sometimes people went into shock. Some became too upset to answer. But if they could speak, the detectives always asked as many questions as possible. When someone died under suspicious circumstances and there was no clear suspect, the only thing the detectives could do was work backwards. Where had the victim been before he died? Who had been with him? Who was the last person to see him alive? Who had a reason to want him dead?

"There was a reception afterwards, but Edwin excused himself," Mrs. Sloane said. "He told everyone that he wasn't feeling well. But he told me he was going to the office and that he'd meet me at home."

He had left the store around nine-thirty, she said. That made sense to the detectives. It would have taken Scarr about ten minutes to drive from the bookstore to his office building. Allow a few minutes for parking, and that agreed with what Lorenzo Rego had told them earlier. The cleaner had seen Mr. Scarr in the elevator at a quarter to ten.

"Who was at the party?"

There were forty or fifty people there, Mrs. Sloane said. Some were from By the Book's head office. Some were reporters. Anna Farrow, a book reviewer for a national newspaper, was there.

"I saw Edwin speaking with her," Mrs. Sloane said. "And Trevor Hanson, President of By the Book. It was his idea to launch Edwin's latest book in the store. Sara and James were there, too, of course."

Sara Mystinski was Scarr's literary agent, she explained. James Afton was a business associate.

"He and Edwin worked together on spin-offs of Edwin's books," Mrs. Sloane said.

Detective Anthony was making detailed notes.

"Spin-offs?"

"Edwin's books were wildly popular," Mrs. Sloane said. "Kids couldn't get enough of them. James came up with the idea of selling accessories — book lights so kids could read in bed after lights out, glow-in-the-dark pen and pencil sets, bookmarks, stickers — all associated with the books. Edwin was pleased by his success, but he was a little embarrassed, too."

"Embarrassed?" Uncle Joe found that hard to believe.

"He worried that people didn't take him seriously. Anna Farrow called his books trash." Tears welled up in her eyes. "Edwin took that hard."

The detectives asked whether Scarr had spoken to anyone besides Anna Farrow.

"He spoke to Dylan," Mrs. Sloane said.

Dylan Dumont was Scarr's twenty-year-old son from his first marriage. He had arrived in town the day before the launch. Scarr hadn't seen him since the boy was eleven years old. It had been a bitter divorce. Scarr's first wife had won sole custody of the boy. Scarr was able to see him for only two weeks each summer. Mrs. Sloane said that Dylan's mother had poisoned the boy against his father. After a few years, Dylan had refused to visit anymore. Then, suddenly, he had appeared in town.

"How did he and his father get along?"

"Not well. They exchanged heated words at the launch."

"Do you know what it was about?"

She shook her head.

"Edwin told me the boy resented him for being an absent father. Edwin invited him to the launch, but he didn't think Dylan would attend. Then, part-way through the evening, I saw Dylan go up to Edwin and grab his arm. But I couldn't hear what they were saying."

"Did you call your husband when you got home?" Detective Anthony asked.

She shook her head. Scarr never answered the phone when he was working. Even if he heard it ring, he never checked his voice mail.

"He always said that telephones and e-mail are fine when you want to reach out and touch someone, but that he didn't like being poked by people all day every day," she said.

"Did your husband own a gun?" Uncle Joe asked.

Mrs. Sloane looked startled. "I don't think so."

"You're not certain?"

"We've been married for less than two years," she said. "Edwin had forty-three years of living before we met. We all have our secrets, Detective. But I don't think a gun was one of Edwin's."

The detectives made a note to check the gun registry. Then they asked if Scarr had life insurance.

"Yes, of course." Mrs. Sloane admitted that she was the beneficiary.

"Did he have a will?"

Mrs. Sloane frowned. "Why are you asking me these questions? Surely you don't think that I — "

"I know it's hard for you, Mrs. Sloane," Uncle Joe said. "But we have to ask."

Yes, she said, Scarr had written a will that left almost everything to her. She now controlled his business interests and the copyrights to all his books. He had also left his son a million dollars.

Detective Anthony noted this. She would double-check with Mr. Scarr's lawyer. Then she closed her memo book and offered to call someone who could stay with Mrs. Sloane.

Still trembling, Mrs. Sloane decided to make the call herself. The detectives waited until a friend arrived. Before they left, they gave Mrs. Sloane their cards with their phone numbers and told her that they would arrange for her to get to the morgue to identify her husband. Mrs. Sloane collapsed against her friend and sobbed.

• • •

"It's never easy," Uncle Joe said. "And the worst part is that while you're feeling sorry for the person, part of your brain is wondering, did she do it? Have I just had a conversation with a murderer?"

"Did she do it?" I asked.

"Have you ever heard the expression, there's no such thing as a free lunch?"

I had.

"Well, I'm hungry," Uncle Joe said. "How do you feel about pancakes and maple syrup?"

I said I felt pretty good about them.

"Terrific," Uncle Joe said. "The cookbook is on the shelf beside the fridge."

"What cookbook?"

"The one with the pancake recipe in it. You mix 'em, I'll cook 'em."

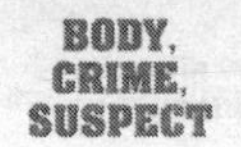

"I don't know how to mix pancakes."

"That's why there are recipes. And I have a great dessert planned," he added.

"What?"

"The real deal on autopsies."

Yum, yum.

QUESTIONS, QUESTIONS, QUESTIONS[6]

When the suspect is unknown, homicide investigators get leads by gathering and analyzing information about the victim. Who was he? Did he have any problems? Any enemies? Is there anything in his past that might explain what happened? Homicide detectives talk to many people and ask many questions. Some of the things they ask about are:

The circumstances surrounding the death

- When was the victim last seen alive? Where? By whom?
- Where was the victim before he died? What was he doing? Who was he with?

The victim's medical records

- Did the victim have medical problems that might have contributed to his death?
- Is there anything in Emergency Medical Service records — for example, ambulance or paramedic records — that could be useful?
- Was the victim taking any medication?
- Was he being treated by a doctor for any medical condition?

The victim's life and personal history

- Was he married, single or divorced? If married, to whom? For how long? If divorced, from whom? For how long?
- What other family did he have — parents, siblings, children, other relatives?
- What was his family background?
- Where did he work? For how long had he worked there? What was his work history? Did he have any problems at work?
- Did the victim have a lot of money? Did he have financial problems?
- What were the victim's daily routines, habits and activities?
- Who were his friends and associates?
- What was his educational background?
- Did the victim have a criminal record?

CHAPTER 7

The Body Reveals Secrets After Death

THE PANCAKES WERE GREAT, but I think that had more to do with how Uncle Joe cooked them than with how I mixed them. The pure Quebec maple syrup didn't hurt, either. I tried to get Uncle Joe to keep talking while we were eating, but he made me wait.

"Autopsies don't make good table talk," he said.

I could imagine. "I guess you're glad they're someone else's job," I said.

"What do you mean?"

"I mean, I guess you're glad you don't have to go to autopsies."

"If that's your guess," Uncle Joe said, "then you're wrong."

"You'd like to have to go to autopsies?"

"I do have to go to autopsies."

"How come?" I asked.

"First things first," Uncle Joe said.

• • •

The morning following the murder, Uncle Joe paid a visit to the crime lab. He had with him the carefully packaged and sealed cartridge case and the one bullet found at the crime scene. He asked to speak to Peter Westcott, one of the lab's firearms examiners. He explained what had happened and asked if Westcott could examine the items and tell him what kind of gun had fired them.

Westcott concentrated on the cartridge case. Identifying its calibre would be relatively easy. Every cartridge case had a head stamp on it — a marking on its base that identifies the manufacturer and calibre. By examining this, Westcott could tell what type of ammunition it was and generally what kind of gun it had been fired from. He could also examine the bullet and cartridge case, and the marks the gun had left on them. Comparing these to others in the lab's reference collection could tell him the type of gun that could have fired them. In this case, he told Uncle Joe that the murder weapon was probably a Browning Hi-Power, Model 1935, 9-mm parabellum/luger calibre.

"It's a semi-automatic with a thirteen-shot-capacity magazine," he said.

But where was the gun?

Dr. Emily Greenwood arrived at work to find that she had been assigned Edwin Scarr's case. Dr. Greenwood was a medical doctor who specialized in forensic pathology. Pathology is the study of the causes of injury and disease. Forensic pathologists are experts in interpreting injuries. They can determine the cause of death, the type of weapon used and whether the death was a homicide or suicide. They arrive at their conclusions by doing postmortem examinations, or autopsies. The purpose of an autopsy is to observe the body and to make a permanent legal record of it.

Edwin Scarr's autopsy was scheduled for the afternoon following his death.

Present at the autopsy were Dr. Greenwood, two pathology assistants, Uncle Joe and Detective Anthony,

Officer Durning from the Forensic Identification Unit and Peter Westcott, the firearms examiner. Each had a special role to play.

Dr. Greenwood was in charge. Her job was to examine the body and answer questions related to the death.

The homicide detectives were there to observe in case anything important was discovered. They could also answer any questions Dr. Greenwood might have about the victim or the circumstances.

As the Ident officer, Officer Durning would fingerprint the deceased. That would help him eliminate some of the fingerprints he had found at the crime scene. He would photograph the victim at each stage of the postmortem. He would take pictures of the body before and after the clothing was removed. If the bullet had passed through several layers of clothing, he would label and take a picture of each hole before the piece of clothing was removed. He would also take close-ups of each bullet hole, wound, injury and mark on the body — placing a small ruler alongside to show the size of each wound or mark. Finally, he would take possession of evidence — the victim's clothing, any bullets that might be recovered and any samples that might be sent for examination. He was in charge of packaging each item, labelling it, sealing it and transporting it to the crime lab.

Peter Westcott, the firearms examiner, was there to help do a preliminary examination of the clothing and the bullet wounds. When a bullet passes through a human body, it makes entrance wounds and exit wounds. By examining the bullet wounds, an expert might be able to figure out the type of weapon used, the kind of ammunition, the firing range (how far the victim was from the firearm) and the direction and angle of fire.

There are many steps to an autopsy. Each must be done with care.

First, Dr. Greenwood asked the detectives what they knew about what had happened. This would give her an idea of what she might be looking at. It was important for her to know in this case that no firearm had been found at the scene. This suggested that Scarr's death had not been suicide.

Because the victim had been shot, the body was X-rayed before it was brought into the autopsy suite. The X-rays would show if there were any bullets or bullet fragments in the body and, if so, where they were. These would have to be removed carefully, without causing damage, and turned over to forensic experts for examination.

When the body was brought in, it was in exactly the same condition as it had been when Lorenzo Rego had found it. It was in a plastic pouch, or "body bag," which had been sealed. Nothing had been removed or altered.

First Dr. Greenwood examined the clothing. She looked for tears or holes made by the bullets. She also looked for firearms discharge residue (unburned or partly burned powder on the clothing or body) that could help to show how far the victim had been from the gun. She looked for any other rips on the clothing that might tell her that there had been a struggle. Then, layer by layer, the clothes were removed. Each item was separately packaged, labelled and sealed by Officer Durning.

Next, Dr. Greenwood weighed and measured the body. This is standard procedure for any autopsy. She looked carefully at every part of the body and made a note of all distinguishing marks: wounds, injuries like bruises or scratches and signs of disease. Whenever she found something, she made a note of its location. She used a series of printed forms that showed outlines of the body — the hands, the front, back and sides of the body, and the front, side and top views of the skull. Every mark and wound was also photographed and measured. By exam-

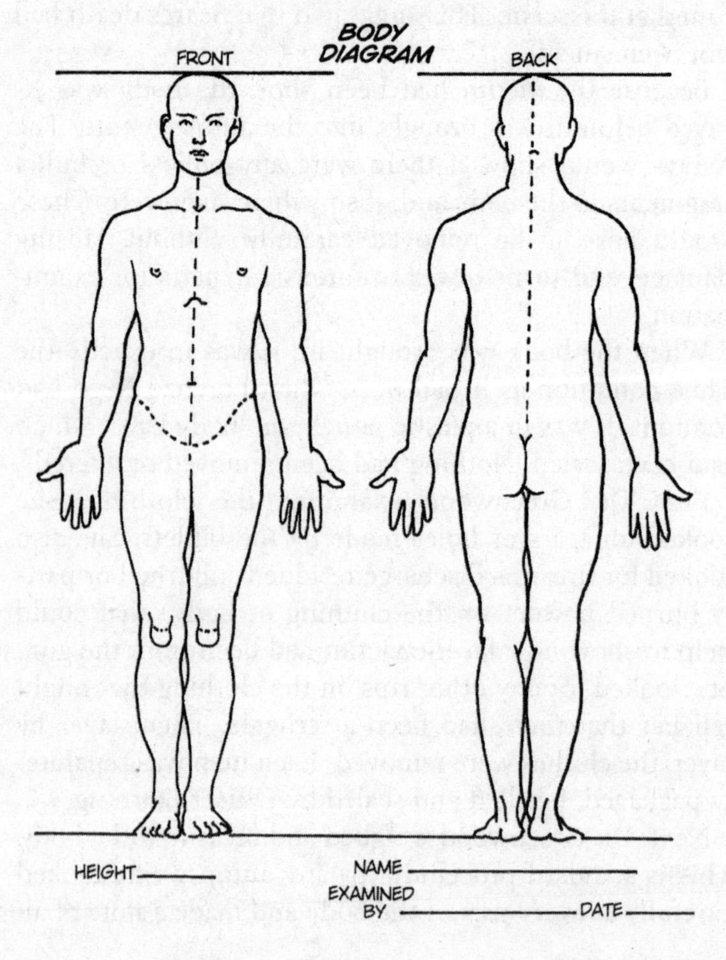

ining these marks, a pathologist can tell if they were caused when the victim tried to defend himself.

She paid special attention to the two bullet wounds. When a bullet hits a body, it's usually still intact and hasn't yet expanded. Because of this, it makes a smaller hole going in than it does when it leaves the body. It's possible to roughly figure out the calibre of the bullet from the entry wound. A bullet entering the body leaves a bruise called a "contusion ring" that can show the direction from which it was fired. The skin around the bullet hole is often scorched or burned by gunpowder. The degree of scorching — a little or a lot — can give information about the distance from which the gun was fired. The closer the gun was to the body when it was fired, the more scorching there is.

One bullet had gone through the body, leaving an entry and an exit wound. That made sense. Officer Durning had found a bullet at the scene. The second bullet had made only an entry wound and was still inside. The X-ray showed where it was.

Dr. Greenwood also inspected the victim's clothing and body for signs of trace evidence: paint flecks, tiny pieces of glass, fibres, blood or hairs.

After the clothes had been removed and the outside of the body examined in detail, Dr. Greenwood did the rest of the autopsy. She examined all the organs. It was important to do a thorough examination. Sometimes it turned out that a person who had been badly injured had not died because of these injuries, but from another cause, such as a heart attack. She traced the path of the bullets and recovered the bullet that was still inside the body. What she found was somewhat unexpected.

Peter Westcott stepped forward to take a closer look. He had been doing his job for a long time and had developed an encyclopedic knowledge of firearms and ammunition. He explained to the police officers that this bullet was different from the one found at the crime scene. The first one was a jacketed round-nose bullet. The one Dr. Greenwood had just removed was a hollow-point lead bullet.

"Does that mean two guns?" Detective Anthony asked.

"Until I have both cartridge cases or examine both bullets, I can't tell you for certain," Westcott said. It was possible for two different bullet types to be fired from one gun, but he would have to compare them to be sure.

The detectives looked at Officer Durning. The Ident officer would have to intensify the search for the second cartridge case.

Then Dr. Greenwood took samples of blood, urine, stomach contents and the liver. These would be sent to the lab for a toxicology examination. This was also standard procedure.

After completing the autopsy, Dr. Greenwood would write a detailed report. It was clear that in this case the cause of death had been two close-range gunshot wounds to the chest. Her opinion: homicide.

Chapter 8
The Investigation Continues

"CAN I ASK YOU something, Uncle Joe?"

"Shoot."

I was learning what a comedian my uncle was. "Very funny."

He shrugged. "What's the question?"

"Did you ever get around to some real detective work? You know, talking to witnesses? Locating some good suspects? That kind of stuff?"

Uncle Joe poured himself a second cup of coffee and filled me in.

• • •

When a murder is first discovered, the investigation focuses on the body and the crime scene, he said. But if an arrest isn't made right away, the focus starts to shift. The homicide detectives have to interview dozens of witnesses. Time can be critical. They want to catch the murderer before he or she flees. Often other police officers get involved and are assigned specific tasks. Someone has to coordinate their activity. A clerk is assigned to keep track of witness statements.

Fourteen hours after Edwin Scarr's body was discovered, the police had done a thorough investigation of the crime scene and of the victim. The pathologist had determined the cause of death. But no eyewitnesses had been found. And there was still no answer to the most important question: Who killed Edwin Scarr?

Many things had to happen before the question could be answered.

First, the homicide detectives had to find people who knew the victim, who had seen him or spoken to him in the hours leading up to his death, or who might know something about who had killed him and why.

Second, a canvass had to be organized of the area surrounding the building where the murder had been committed. Police officers would go door-to-door and business-to-business to see if anyone had seen or heard anything that might help.

Third, the Forensic Identification unit had to finish its work at the crime scene and find the second cartridge case.

Fourth, items recovered at the crime scene had to be sent to the crime lab for analysis.

After speaking with the victim's widow, the detectives drew up a preliminary list of people to speak with. They began to contact these people. Over the next few days, they asked many questions to try to uncover who had spoken to Scarr that night and what they had said. They wanted to know if anyone had been seen leaving the book launch with Scarr or shortly afterwards. Had anyone been seen going into the Belmont around the same time as Scarr? They needed more information on Scarr himself and on anyone who would profit from his death. Every interview had to be documented. This was a painstaking effort.

The interviews began.

The bookstore owner

Trevor Henson was president of the By the Book bookstore chain where Edwin Scarr's book launch had been held. The detectives found him in his office downtown. Henson told the detectives that nothing unusual had happened that night, except that he had seen Scarr arguing with his son, Dylan. Henson didn't know much about Dylan or where the detectives could find him.

Henson also told the detectives that Scarr was supposed to meet some of Henson's business associates at the party following the book launch. Henson had been working on a deal for a special Edwin Scarr feature on the chain's Web site. But just before the launch, Scarr told Henson that he had changed his mind. He didn't want to be on the Web site after all. When Henson asked why, Scarr said that he was making changes in his life — big changes — and that the Web site wouldn't fit in. He wouldn't tell Henson what the changes were.

Hensen admitted that he was angry and disappointed. He had found some big sponsors for the site. He had been planning to make an announcement the next day. He also admitted that he had left the book launch early to tell the sponsors that the deal was off. He had left alone and gone straight to his home office.

Did he have an alibi?

"I was on the phone for three hours solid with sponsors in Calgary, Vancouver, New York, Chicago and Seattle," he said. "Does that count?"

When Detective Anthony asked for the names and phone numbers of the people he had spoken to, Henson had his secretary print a list off the computer. The detectives took it. They would check it out.

The agent

Next the detectives visited Scarr's agent, Sara Mystinski. Trevor Henson had told them that Scarr owed most of his success to Sara. In five short years, she had negotiated multi-million dollar deals for him, making him one of the most successful children's writers in the world. The detectives found Mystinski at her office in a trendy part of town.

Mystinski told the detectives that she had been at the book launch from the beginning until "the bitter end."

"It was a zoo," she said. "There were hundreds of children there. They all wanted Edwin's autograph. He spoke to every one of them."

Did she notice if anything seemed to be bothering Mr. Scarr?

No, she said. In fact, he seemed to be in a better-than-usual mood for most of the evening. He even chatted with Anna Farrow, the book critic.

"Was that unusual?" Detective Anthony asked.

"You bet it was," Mystinski said. Scarr had always resented the fact that Anna Farrow refused to review his books. "She thought Edwin was some kind of evil influence on kids," she said. No, she didn't know what Scarr and Anna Farrow had chatted about. Trevor Henson told her at the party that Scarr had backed out of the Web site deal. When she asked Scarr about it, he said he would tell her everything the next day. She had the feeling something was up, but she didn't know what.

She told the detectives that Edwin's mood changed when his estranged son showed up. Mystinski was surprised to see Dylan at the launch. He and Scarr had lunched together the previous day, and Scarr had told Sara that it hadn't gone well. She saw Dylan and Edwin arguing partway through the evening. She couldn't remember what time that was. Maybe around eight-thirty. She had no idea when Dylan left the store.

Mystinski left the bookstore at about nine-thirty, soon after Scarr. She went straight home to her cat and her canary. She didn't know if anyone had seen her entering her house, which was a ten-minute walk from Scarr's office. She had a shower, got into bed, turned on the television and fell asleep sometime after the late news.

"Do you know if Mr. Scarr owned a gun?" Detective Anthony asked.

"He had one in his office a few years ago. At first I thought it was a fake — you know, a toy. But it wasn't."

"How do you know?"

"He gave it to me to hold. It was heavy. As soon as it was in my hand, he told me it was loaded. I was so scared I just about dropped the darned thing." She shook her head. "Edwin had a strange sense of humour sometimes."

"Do you know where he kept the gun?"

She shook her head. "I never saw it again after that. In fact, I made it pretty clear that I never wanted to see it again."

Before the detectives left her office, Mystinski told them about James Afton. She said he deserved the real credit for Scarr's success. For years, Scarr had aspired to be the new Dr. Seuss. He had cranked out dozens of never-published rhyming books for children. It was Afton who had encouraged him to write horror novels.

"James was working on a deal for a TV series based on Edwin's books," Mystinski said.

The business partner

The detectives found James Afton on the thirteenth floor of the Belmont Building. Part of the office suite was still blocked from access by yellow crime-scene tape. A police officer stood guard to keep everyone out. Before the two detectives went to see Afton, they checked in with the Ident unit. The office had been cleared of papers. The computer that had sat on the desk was gone. The missing cartridge case hadn't yet been found, but Officer Durning was studying a small heating vent in the floor. "It could have fallen down there," he said. The two detectives left him to his work.

Like Edwin Scarr, James Afton had a large office. After the detectives introduced themselves, he sat behind his desk and pulled out a pack of cigarettes. "You don't mind, do you?" he said, lighting one. Then he shook his head. "Can you imagine anything more horrible? Poor Edwin. He comes in to work, and some thug attacks and kills him."

He said he would be happy to answer the detectives' questions. No, Edwin had no enemies. No, he wasn't in any kind of trouble. No, he didn't know that Edwin had decided to pull out of the deal with Trevor Henson and By the Book. In fact, Afton seemed surprised by the question. He said he didn't know anything about changes Edwin may have been planning.

Did Scarr have a gun?

"Why? You don't think he killed himself, do you?"

"We understand he may have had a gun in his office at one time," Detective Anthony said.

"He had some old relic that he liked to play with," Afton said.

"Did he keep it loaded?"

"Loaded? Not that I'm aware of. I told him he should get rid of the thing. I'm not even sure he had a permit for it. He told me he'd found it at his father's place after the old man died. I think his father brought it back from Korea."

"When was the last time you saw the gun?"

Afton shook his head. "It's been quite a while," he said. "In fact, I assumed he'd taken my advice for a change. I thought he'd gotten rid of it."

Could Afton think of anyone who may have wanted to kill Scarr?

"Maybe that son of his," Afton said. "He showed up at the book launch and made a big stink. I saw him yelling at Edwin about something."

Did he have any idea where they could find Dylan Dumont?

"I think Martha came in this morning to get some names and phone numbers for Jennifer," Afton said. "She would know." He butted his cigarette and picked up the telephone. He called Martha Cooper into his office.

"Dylan Dumont phoned here a couple of times, didn't he, Martha?" he said.

Martha Cooper sniffed the air in the office. "May I remind you that this is a non-smoking building, Mr. Afton?" she said sternly.

Afton looked sheepish. "I've been trying to quit," he said. "But at times like this — " He shrugged. "Martha, these officers want to know about Edwin's son."

"Dylan called several times to talk to Mr. Scarr," the secretary said. "He kept asking me to put him through to

Mr. Scarr. He got angry when I said he'd have to leave a message with me."

"Did he say where he was staying?"

"At a youth hostel in the east end," she said. "I wrote the name down somewhere. Would you like me to see if I still have it?"

"If you don't mind," Uncle Joe said.

While Martha Cooper went to look, the detectives asked more questions.

Yes, Afton had been at the book launch. Like Sara Mystinski, he left early, just after Scarr.

"I had a headache. A few hundred kids can be noisy, to say the least," he explained. "I took a walk to clear my head, then drove home."

He had arrived home at eleven o'clock, he said. He told the detectives that he lived alone in a condominium near the waterfront.

Before leaving the office, the detectives stopped at Martha Cooper's desk. They asked her about Edwin Scarr's gun. Yes, she knew he had one, and she didn't approve of it one bit. She had told him to get rid of it. What would his younger readers think if they knew he kept a gun in his desk?

"Do you know where it is now?" Uncle Joe asked.

"I have no idea," Martha Cooper said. "I only saw it once. Thank goodness."

Uncle Joe thought about how the secretary had spoken to Afton.

"Is Mr. Afton also your boss?" he asked.

"He most certainly is not!" she said. "Mr. Scarr was my boss. He only gave Mr. Afton an office here because they've known each other for so long. Mr. Afton's last business went bankrupt two years ago. Since then he's been trying to figure out ways to make money out of Mr. Scarr's books."

"It sounds like you don't approve," Uncle Joe said.

Martha Cooper glanced at the closed door to James Afton's office. She lowered her voice.

"If you ask me, Mr. Afton is one of those people who pick their friends based on what they can get from them. I don't know why Mr. Scarr worked with him." Then she added, "He's one of the most inconsiderate people I've ever met. He knows perfectly well he isn't supposed to smoke in here."

The detectives left with the address of the hostel where Dylan Dumont had been staying. They wondered if he would still be there.

The son

"He checked out this morning," the manager at the hostel told the detectives.

"What time?"

"Around ten." It was now after four in the afternoon.

"Do you know where he went?"

"He said he was catching a seven o'clock train this evening. When he checked out, he asked if he could leave his bag here while he took a walk on the boardwalk." The nearby boardwalk ran along the lake.

"I don't suppose it's still here?" Uncle Joe asked.

"It is. He said he'd pick it up around five."

Uncle Joe asked the clerk for a description of Dylan. Then, while he and his partner waited in their car for him to return, they discussed the case. They didn't have enough information yet to develop a theory. But they were interested in Dylan because he had reappeared in Scarr's life suddenly just before the murder. He had been seen arguing with Scarr the night of the murder. He stood to gain from Scarr's death — he would inherit a million dollars. He obviously had a grudge against Scarr. Had the grudge and the inheritance given him a motive for murder?

Soon a young man came up the street toward the hostel. He matched the description the clerk had given them. The two detectives stopped him.

"Dylan Dumont?" Uncle Joe said. The young man turned toward him. He didn't look surprised when the detectives introduced themselves.

"This is about Edwin Sloane, isn't it?" Dylan asked. The detectives noted that he did not refer to Scarr as his father.

"Yes, it is. We'd like you to come down to the station with us so we can talk to you."

"Are you arresting me?"

"We just want to ask you some questions."

"I have a train to catch."

"This shouldn't take long," Uncle Joe said.

Dylan agreed to go with them, but the detectives could tell that he wasn't happy about it. At the station, they took him into a small interview room and explained that they were going to videotape his statement. This seemed to make Dylan nervous.

"You think I killed him, don't you?"

"We're trying to find out happened," Uncle Joe said. "Videotaping is standard procedure. Now, Dylan, what can you tell us about your father?"

"What's to tell?" Dylan said. He said that his parents

had divorced when he was five years old. For a few years, Dylan saw his father for two weeks each summer. Then, when he was eleven, he decided he didn't want to see him any more.

"We had nothing in common," Dylan said. "You can't get to know a person you only see for a few days each year. Besides, Mom remarried and Steve — my stepfather — was more of a dad to me than Edwin Sloane ever was."

"What brought you to town, Dylan?"

"Curiosity. I'd heard a lot about him lately."

He added that his stepfather had died the previous year. Things were hard for his mother now. She had quit her job to nurse her husband, became depressed after he died and now was living on what she could earn as a house cleaner.

"It was the only job she could get," Dylan said bitterly. "And it looks like I'm going to have to drop out of university. We don't have the money to pay the tuition. I thought if I explained this to Edwin, he might help us out. I spent the last of my textbook money on train fare and a crummy hostel."

"Did he help you out?"

"I didn't ask him," Dylan said.

He said that he had arrived in town the day before the book launch. He had to call Scarr's office several times before he managed to speak to his father. Scarr invited him out to lunch.

"He didn't even ask about Mom. He didn't seem very interested in me, either. So I didn't ask him for anything. I didn't want to beg for a handout."

"What can you tell us about the book launch?" Detective Anthony said.

"What about it?"

"Why were you there?"

"He invited me. I wasn't going to go. Then, that night, I went out for a walk and suddenly there was the store where the launch was happening. I went in."

Dylan said he had watched his father signing books and chatting with his young fans. He got along so well with them. It made Dylan angry that his father seemed to care more for his young readers than he did for his own son. Dylan said he had planned to leave without speaking to his father, but Scarr saw him and came over to him. Yes, Dylan admitted, they had argued. Dylan had told his father exactly what he thought of him. Then he had left the store because "there was no reason to stay."

He didn't go back to the hostel immediately. Instead, he walked around town for an hour or two "to calm down." No, he didn't speak to anyone, nor did he stop into any stores to buy anything.

"Do you know if your father owned a gun, Dylan?"

"I know he had one about ten years ago." One summer, Dylan had been playing around in the attic of the cottage that had belonged to his grandfather. He had found an old trunk. There was a gun in it. "Edwin freaked when he saw me with it. Turned out it was loaded, but I didn't know it at the time. He took the gun away and told me to stay out of the attic. I told him it was all his fault — he shouldn't keep a loaded gun around."

"Do you know what happened to it?"

"That was the last summer I saw him — until a couple of days ago."

Dylan told the detectives he hadn't known about his father's will.

The book critic

The two detectives found Anna Farrow at her home in the west end of the city.

"I heard the news," she said. "Who could have done such a thing?"

"We understand you were at Mr. Scarr's book launch and that you spoke to him," Uncle Joe said. "What can you tell us about that?"

The critic said that when she received the invitation, she had tossed it into the garbage. There were so many books published each year, she said. She felt her job was to tell readers about the best of children's literature, not the worst.

"Then why did you go to the launch?" Detective Anthony asked.

"Edwin called me personally and invited me. He said he thought I would have a special interest in witnessing what he called the end of an era."

"End of an era?"

"That's what he said. Naturally I was intrigued. I went. The book he was launching was another in his endless stream of second-rate horror novels. But he came over to me and told me I would hear from him first thing the next morning and that I would be interested in what he had to say. He said it would surprise everyone, even his wife. Of course, I never did hear from him."

"Do you have any idea what he was referring to?"

The critic shook her head. "He wouldn't tell me. He just said he was going to knock my socks off."

Farrow left the store shortly after nine, right after speaking to Scarr. She arrived home at about nine-thirty. Her husband was there, reading and listening to music.

She didn't seem to mind when the detectives asked for her husband's name and business address and phone number.

The canvass

While the detectives were conducting interviews, other police officers were canvassing the area around the Belmont Building. The area was filled with stores and design studios. Most of them had been closed between the time Edwin Scarr was last seen alive and the time he was found dead. But there were also artists' studios, small restaurants, fast-food outlets, convenience stores and a gas station in the neighbourhood. Police visited each establishment to ask if anyone had seen anything unusual the night of the murder. They also checked out which buildings and businesses had security cameras, and asked for any videotapes that may have been made that night.

There was an apartment building across the street from the Belmont. Some of the apartments faced the window to Scarr's office. Two teams of police officers knocked on doors and asked tenants if they had seen anything.

By all accounts, nobody who lived or worked in the area had seen anything out of the ordinary on the night that Edwin Scarr was murdered.

Other interviews

Other police officers were sent to find everyone who had attended the book launch. Most of the children had come with at least one parent. Dozens of people had attended the party after the launch. There were also store employees and extra security guards on duty that evening. The police wanted to speak to everyone who might have seen or heard something that could be helpful. Every interview had to be conducted carefully. Notes had to be taken. The names and addresses of each person had to be recorded. At this point, the officers weren't sure what might turn out to be important. They worked slowly and carefully.

They also located a publicist for the bookstore who put them in touch with a photographer who had shot several rolls of film that night. The police would contact the photographer for copies of the pictures.

Back at the crime scene

Officer Durning was determined to find that second cartridge case — if it existed. He had found out at the postmortem examination that two different bullets had been fired. This was unusual. It could mean that two guns had been used. Officer Durning didn't think this was likely, but he was careful not to jump to conclusions. Two guns could mean two killers or two suspects involved in the killing. Finding and examining the second cartridge case would help police reach a definite conclusion.

It made no sense that someone would fire two shots, pick up one cartridge case and leave the second behind. But again, Officer Durning was careful not to jump to conclusions. Maybe the killer had been smart enough to know that the cartridge cases were important. Maybe he had retrieved one of them, but had been interrupted in his search for the second one. Or maybe that second case was still somewhere in the office. Officer Durning thought this made the most sense.

He searched every square centimetre of carpet. He

searched each piece of furniture. He checked the file drawers that had been open when the body was discovered. Nothing. He inspected the heating vent on the floor. It was covered with a grille. The spaces in the grille looked large enough for a cartridge case to slip through.

Carefully, Officer Durning loosened the grille from the vent. He peered inside with his flashlight. He saw nothing. He noticed a twist in the shaft. Something — a cartridge case — could have fallen into the grille and slipped down the shaft. But how far would it fall? Where would it end up?

It was time to call Building Maintenance.

Officer Durning kept an officer posted at the door while he went in search of answers.

• • •

"And?" I asked.

"And what?"

"Who was it? It was the son, right? He hated his dad. He knew about the gun. He had been seen arguing with him right before the murder. He was going to inherit a million dollars. It had to be him."

"He looked good for it," Uncle Joe said. "But thinking someone did it and proving they did are two completely different things. We had to be able to put the suspect at the scene at the time of the murder. Or we had to tie him to the murder weapon, which we didn't have. We had a lot of puzzle pieces, but so far we didn't know what the puzzle looked like. We didn't even know if all the pieces we had belonged to the puzzle of what happened to Edwin Scarr."

"What did you do?"

Uncle Joe looked at his watch. "I'd better call and see

what's happening with the power and the roads."

"Call later."

"This will just take a minute."

Uncle Joe pulled out his cellphone and made a few calls. He didn't look happy when he pressed "End" and tucked the phone back into his pocket.

"We're socked in for at least another night," he said. "I'm going to start some coffee. You want anything?"

"I want to know what you did next."

Uncle Joe laughed.

Chapter 9

The Crime Lab

"REMEMBER WHAT I TOLD YOU about the Forensic Identification unit?" Uncle Joe said as he put some water on to boil.

I nodded.

"Well, forensic scientists are just as methodical and meticulous as Ident officers. When you start with a crime scene and a few little pieces of evidence, and when you need to have a clear idea of who did what, how they did it and what's important to the case, you have to go slowly. Step by step. You have to be methodical."

• • •

While the police were interviewing witnesses, Uncle Joe said, another team of investigators was on the case. Forensic scientists.

Forensic scientists use their scientific knowledge in the service of the law. Science can help in many kinds of investigations — and many kinds of science can be helpful in understanding how a crime was committed and who may have been responsible.

Forensic scientists are objective in their work. Their role isn't to prove that someone is guilty — or innocent. Their job is to examine items related to a crime and to report their findings accurately. Sometimes these findings are helpful, even critical, in proving who committed the crime. Just as often — and just as importantly their work excludes people as suspects.

There are many experts at work in the crime lab. They include:

Forensic biologists, who examine substances such as blood and saliva and items such as hair and fibres. They use DNA profiling to identify or exclude suspects. They also interpret bloodstain patterns, which can help in understanding what happened at the scene of a crime.

Firearms and toolmarks examiners, who examine weapons, ammunition and tools (for example, tire irons, screwdrivers, pliers and cutters) and the marks made by these items. These are the experts who can match a bullet to the gun that fired it.

Forensic toxicologists, who look for the presence or absence of alcohol, drugs or poisons. Even when a person is shot to death, these findings can be important.

Forensic chemists, who analyze materials like paint, glass, gunshot residue, soil, minerals, metals and plastics. They can tell from which side a piece of glass was broken, match tiny paint fragments found on a hit-and-run victim to the car that hit them and determine what caused the fire that burned down a house.

Forensic photoanalysts, who use cameras, sometimes in combination with microscopes, to make physical comparisons of items such as paper matches, plastic bags and footwear impressions.

There are also forensic scientists who specialize in examining documents for forgeries. Forensic anthropologists can determine the age and identity of old bones. Forensic accountants examine financial records for evidence of fraud.

• • •

"Did all of those people get involved in this case?" I asked.

"No," Uncle Joe said. "But a lot of them did."

• • •

Each piece of evidence collected from a crime scene is handled with extreme care, Uncle Joe said. It's collected in a way that won't damage the item. It's packaged in a way that will preserve the item. Each item is kept separate so that it can't be contaminated by another item. (Remember Locard's theory — "Every contact leaves a trace.") Each item is sealed so that no one can tamper with it between the time it is collected and the time it is analyzed.

Much of the evidence Officer Durning collected was sent to the crime lab. It included the clothing Scarr was wearing when he died, the biological samples (some of the victim's blood, blood collected at the crime scene, specimens collected at the autopsy) and the tapings of hair and fibres. The two cartridge cases that Officer Durning had discovered — the second one deep in the floor vent — and the two bullets also went to the lab.

Other evidence was examined by the police themselves. These included fingerprints, footwear evidence and Edwin Scarr's computer.

The procedure for submitting samples to the lab was strict. A form had to be filled out. It asked for the name of the deceased (in the case of a death investigation) and of the suspect, if there was one. There was space for background information on the case. The police had to list each item submitted and the type of examination they wanted.

All items went first to the Central Receiving Office,

which made sure that everything had been packaged properly. There was no point in examining evidence that had been damaged or contaminated. Central Receiving also made sure that items were properly documented. It was important to have a record of where each piece of evidence had been, who had been responsible for it and who had examined it. When a case finally got to court, police and scientists could be questioned about this. If they couldn't give a satisfactory answer, they could be accused of mishandling evidence or even of tampering with it. That could destroy a whole case.

Each item was tagged with a bar code, which was scanned into the lab's computer database. Every time the item moved from one department to another or from one scientist to another, the item's bar code would be scanned again. This was called "secure transfer." It ensured that the whereabouts of each item was known at all times. All items were kept under lock and key when they weren't being worked on.

The firearms examiner

Peter Westcott now had two bullets: one recovered from Edwin Scarr's body, the other from his office. He also had two cartridge cases: one found under the desk at Scarr's office, the second found trapped in the heating vent. But the murder weapon had not been found. The most that Westcott could do at this point was to tell the police whether or not the two bullets had been fired from the same gun and what type of gun had fired the bullets. Police would then know what kind of weapon they were looking for.

Peter Westcott knew firearms. Specifically, he knew

"small arms" — handguns, rifles and shotguns. (Heavier weapons, such as cannons, missiles and most rockets, are called "artillery.")

Small arms are divided into two categories. Long arms — rifles and shotguns — are shoulder-fired. Handguns are designed to be fired by one hand.

There are three types of handguns.

Manually operated handguns such as single- and double-shot derringers are capable of firing one shot at a time and have to be reloaded or cocked between shots.

Revolvers have rotating cylinders that hold between five and nine cartridges. When a revolver is fired, the cylinder turns to rotate a fresh cartridge into position. When the bullet is fired, the cartridge cases are not ejected. They stay in the cylinder. If someone is killed with a revolver, you won't find cartridges cases at the scene unless the killer opens the gun and ejects them manually.

The third type of handgun is the semi-automatic pistol. Its cartridges are held in a magazine. When a semi-automatic pistol is fired, the cartridge cases are ejected. Unless the shooter picks them up and carries them away, they can be found at the scene of the crime.

Finding more than one cartridge case is critical in proving that two or more shots were fired from the same gun. The cases can also be matched to the specific murder weapon.

To most people, guns are weapons. To Peter Westcott, they're simply tools. As such, they leave "toolmarks" on the parts of a bullet or cartridge case that come into contact with them. Westcott's job is to look at these marks in the same way he might look at those made by a screwdriver that's been used to pry open a window. His science is the identification of matching marks: Did this screwdriver make this mark in this piece of metal? Did this gun make these marks on this particular bullet?

When a gun is fired, a cartridge enters the gun's chamber. A firing pin strikes it, igniting a primer, which in turn ignites the gunpowder. The burning powder sends off a gas that expands in the cartridge. The gas pushes the bullet out of the cartridge case and sends it speeding out through the barrel of the gun. At each of these stages, the gun leaves marks on the case and on the bullet.[7]

What makes these marks?

The inside of a gun barrel is rifled — spiral "lands" and "grooves" are cut into the metal of the barrel. These help to stabilize the bullet by spinning it as it passes through the barrel. They also leave impressions on the bullet that can be used to identify the specific firearm from which a bullet was fired. Different types and makes of guns have different numbers of lands and grooves. The direction of the rifling — whether it spirals or twists to the left or to the right — is also different for different makes of guns. A firearms examiner can check reference books and computer databases to find out which guns of the same calibre have the same number and dimensions of lands and grooves, and which ones have the same direction of "twist."

When the gun's firing pin hits the primer at the base of the cartridge, it also leaves a mark that can be matched back to the firing pin. Other marks are often made on the cartridge case when it is ejected from the chamber of the gun.

First Peter Westcott compared the markings on the bullets and cartridge cases using a comparison microscope

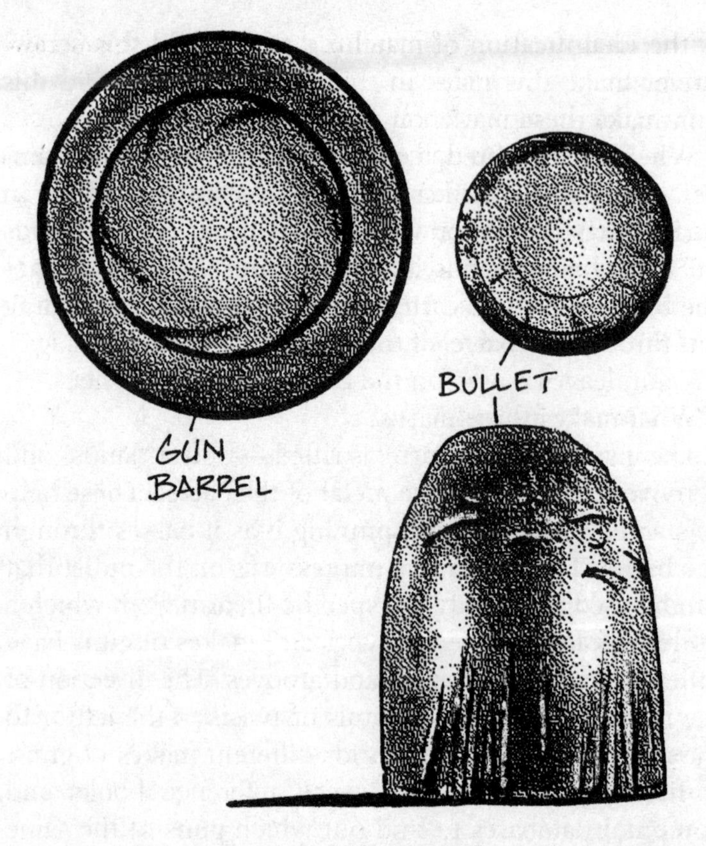

— two microscopes joined by a single optical bridge. As he looked through it, he was able to turn the bullets to try to line up the marks made on them as they passed through the barrel of the gun.

In this case, it wasn't easy. One of the bullets was copper-jacketed. It had clear markings on it. But the other was lead, which is a relatively soft metal. It had struck a bone in the body and been deformed. Westcott found only one small area on the lead bullet that matched markings on the copper-jacketed bullet. It wasn't enough to let him say with certainty that both bullets had been fired from the same gun.

Next he compared the marks on the two cartridge cases. This time he had no doubt. Both had come from the same gun, a Browning Hi-Power, Model 1935, as he had already told the police.

When the murder weapon was found — if it ever was found — Westcott would be able to match it to the bullets and the cartridge cases.

The forensic biologist

Among the items Officer Durning submitted to the crime lab were a sample of the victim's blood; articles of clothing worn by the victim, some of which had blood on them; blood from the carpet in the victim's office; a shoe worn by the cleaner who had found the body, on which there appeared to be blood; the two small drops of blood found on the carpet outside of James Afton's office; some papers with blood on them; and the computer cord with what appeared to be blood on its plug. The question for the biologist was simple — did all of these blood samples come from the same person — the victim — or was there also blood present from a second, unknown person?

The Ident officer had also submitted tapings of fibres collected at the scene. These might prove useful, but at the moment they were not a priority.

The biologist turned her attention to the blood samples. She would extract DNA from each one and produce DNA profiles.

DNA is the genetic blueprint of life. With the exception of identical twins, no two individuals have the same DNA. By comparing DNA profiles from each sample, the biologist would be able to tell if all the blood came from the same person. She could also tell whether the blood came from a male or a female.

The work had to be done carefully. The good news was that DNA technology had become so sophisticated that scientists could produce a DNA profile from a minute amount of blood. Only 40 blood cells — an amount invisible to the naked eye — would be enough. The bad news was that there was always a danger of contamination. This could happen if proper procedures weren't followed while a sample was collected or analyzed.

The lab's computer database contained DNA profiles of everyone who worked at the lab — the scientists, the assistants, even the cleaning staff. When profiles from the crime scene were ready, they would be compared to all the samples in the database. If there had been any accidental contamination by lab staff, that would be shown immediately. The database also contained DNA profiles from people involved in all the other crimes that the lab had worked on.

If the blood found at the Scarr crime scene revealed DNA from anyone besides the victim, that could help the police. When the police finally arrested a suspect, the suspect's DNA could be compared to the unknown DNA profile from the crime scene. If it matched, this could help the police prove that the suspect had been at the scene. Unknown profiles were also compared to the database to see if those profiles had been present at any other crime scene.

All of this would take time, however. The lab was extremely busy. It would be two weeks, at the very least, before the police got their answer.

The forensic toxicologist

Even though Edwin Scarr had been shot to death, samples from his body were sent to a forensic toxicologist. The toxicologist analyzed them for evidence of drugs and alcohol. This was done in all suspicious or unexplained deaths.

In Scarr's case, the toxicologist might find nothing that would help the police homicide investigation. But her findings could become important when a suspect was arrested and the case went to trial.

For example, Mr. Pink kills Mr. Green. Mr. Pink may argue that Mr. Green was under the influence of drugs or alcohol, which caused him to act violently. Mr. Pink claims he had no choice but to kill Mr. Green in self-defense. If the toxicologist's examination shows no trace of drugs or alcohol in Mr. Green, Mr. Pink would be proved a liar.

Another example: Mr. Pink admits that he killed Mr. Green, but claims the killing was not planned and deliberate. He says he killed Mr. Green in a fit of rage. Instead of being charged with first-degree murder, Mr. Pink might face the charge of second-degree murder. But the toxicologist's examination shows evidence of such a high concentration of drugs or alcohol in Mr. Green's system that Mr. Green must have been unconscious when he was killed. The prosecutor would then argue that the murder had been cold-blooded and premeditated. Mr. Pink would be charged with first-degree murder.

In addition to checking for alcohol and illegal drugs, the toxicologist also looked for the presence of any prescription or over-the-counter medication that might cause the victim to be less alert or to fall unconscious.

Normally, she did this by analyzing a blood sample. Other samples had been submitted after the autopsy — urine and samples of the victim's liver and stomach contents. This was routine. They would be used if they were needed, but they weren't always used. It depended on the case and the condition of each type of sample.

Does this match that?

Examination of physical evidence often tries to answer the question: do these two items match in some way? Was the footprint found at the crime scene made by the suspect's shoe? Did the fibres found in the suspect's car come from the carpet at the crime scene? Was the pry mark found on the door frame at the crime scene made by the crowbar that was found at the suspect's house? Was the bullet found in the victim's body fired by the gun that was found in the suspect's house?

This is done by making comparisons. There are two kinds of comparisons.

Comparisons of class characteristics. All Brand X sneakers have the same shape and tread design on the bottom. Brand Y sneakers have a different shape and tread design. Someone familiar with sneakers could probably identify which are Brand X and which are Brand Y by looking at these shape and tread characteristics. These are called class characteristics. They are unique to a specific make or brand of item — and all items of that brand or make share those characteristics. But there could be millions of Brand X sneakers and Brand Y sneakers in existence.

Comparisons of individual characteristics. These are unique to one specific item. Individual characteristics usually develop as a result of wear. No two items wear in exactly the same way. You and a friend may have identical pairs of Brand X sneakers. But you walk everywhere in your sneakers, while your friend's preferred mode of travel is a scooter. Your friend has a puppy that loves to chew on his sneakers. Your hamster pretty much leaves yours alone. Each pair of sneakers develops different individual characteristics that make them easy to identify — even though they started out exactly the same.

YOUR INDIVIDUAL BLUEPRINT[8]

DNA stands for deoxyribonucleic acid. It is often called the "blueprint of the body" because DNA determines all of an individual's inherited characteristics. Each person has DNA from his or her mother and father. With the exception of identical twins, each person's DNA makeup is unique.

DNA is found in the nucleus of every cell in the human body. Each cell contains the same DNA. This means that forensic scientists can use samples of blood, saliva — even the root of a single hair — to develop a DNA profile of a person.

The human body contains about 80 trillion cells — that's 80,000,000,000,000. A forensic scientist needs less than one-billionth of one gram — called 1 ng — to do a DNA analysis. The root sheath of a single hair on your body contains between 10 and 500 ng of DNA — more than enough to generate your DNA profile.

Chapter 10
Narrowing the Investigation

"SO YOU SAT BACK and let the lab experts do their tests," I said. "The firearms guy identified the murder weapon, the biologist told you whose DNA she found, and then the toxicologist told you that Scarr had really been poisoned — something like that?"

"Nothing like that," Uncle Joe said. "The firearms examiner told us what type of gun we were looking for, but we hadn't found it and didn't know where to look for it. The biologist could tell us she'd found the victim's DNA — she compared samples from the crime scene to samples from Scarr. But she couldn't tell us who else's DNA she may have found unless that person was already on a database. Most people aren't. And DNA analysis takes weeks. And, no, he wasn't poisoned. In fact, there was no trace of drugs or alcohol in him."

"So you were right back where you started," I said.

"Not exactly," Uncle Joe said. "We weren't sitting around twiddling our thumbs."

• • •

While the detectives waited for information from the crime lab, they stepped up their investigation.

They wondered if Scarr's computer could tell them anything. First, there was something that looked like blood on the plug. The computer was on the opposite side of the office from the body. No other blood had been found near it, either under the desk or on the carpet or on the power bar. If it was blood, how had it got there? And was it the victim's blood or the killer's? The crime lab would be able to tell them.

Second, why had someone shut off the computer by yanking the cord instead of shutting off the power bar? Had the killer done this while ransacking the office? Had he or she been looking for something? Or had the killer been trying to make murder look like robbery gone wrong? The detectives had rejected the idea that Edwin Scarr had been shot when he surprised an intruder. Blood had been found on the undersides of the papers scattered from the filing cabinets. This meant that they had fallen onto the blood instead of the other way around. The shooting had come before the looting.

Third, they wondered about the "big change" Scarr had been planning. Trevor Henson had told them that Scarr had backed out of a business deal because of it. Scarr had told Anna Farrow that his latest book was "the end of an era." But no one, not even Scarr's wife, knew what the change was. Maybe there was a clue in his computer.

The detectives got a warrant to search the computer's hard drive. The police department's commercial crime section would examine it.

While they waited for the results, they appealed to the public. They briefly described the circumstances of Scarr's death. They asked to be contacted by anyone who had seen anything in or near the Belmont Building that night, or knew anything that might help them to find the killer or the missing murder weapon.

They continued their investigation into Edwin's Scarr's life. They reviewed all of the witness statements that had been gathered from the neighbourhood canvass and from people who had been at the bookstore on the night of the book launch. It was painstaking work. But it yielded results.

A woman had seen Scarr in a heated argument with someone as she was leaving the bookstore. She didn't know the other man, but she recognized him from the launch. To the detectives' surprise, the man she described was not Dylan Dumont. Instead, she had seen an older man, taller than Scarr, with dark hair and a slender build. He was wearing a black leather jacket, black pants and a grey shirt.

A bookstore employee told a similar story. The employee had been packing up a display table while the last children were leaving the store. The invited guests had already moved to the store's second floor for wine and cheese. The first floor, where the launch had taken place, was almost deserted. Edwin Scarr was there, arguing with another man. The employee didn't know what it was about. She gave the police the same description that the first woman had.

Both had described James Afton, Scarr's business partner. The detectives wondered what the two men had been arguing about. They also wondered why Afton hadn't mentioned this to them. They decided to wait before going back to speak with him again. They needed more information.

Then they got another break. Henry Tyrell from the commercial crime section asked them to drop by. He had been examining Scarr's computer.

Tyrell was what you'd expect from a computer expert. He was young and enthusiastic, with an office piled high with manuals, disks, back-up tapes — and computers. He had six or seven of them, different makes and models.

"I can tell you when the plug was yanked," he told the detectives. "It was exactly 11:03 the night of the murder."

"How do you know?" Detective Anthony asked.

Tyrell explained that the computer had to be shut down according to certain procedures. If those procedures weren't followed — because of a power outage or a system crash, for example — this information was stored in a special log by the computer. He showed the detectives the log on Scarr's computer. Sure enough, it had been improperly shut down at 11:03 PM, on the last night of Edwin Scarr's life.

"Could that happen because someone yanked the plug?" Uncle Joe asked.

"Yup."

"What else did you find?'

"A lot of what you'd expect," Tyrell said. "A couple of complete manuscripts from already-published books. He cranked out three books a year, you know." When Detective Anthony looked surprised, Tyrell shrugged. "I have a kid brother who devours his stuff."

"Did you find anything to indicate he was planning a big change in his life?"

Henry Tyrell broke into a broad grin. "Like maybe the manuscript for a book of poetry? Or a letter he was planning to send to the major dailies in the country telling them that he was through with horror? Or how about a letter to a major TV production company telling them that he'd changed his mind about doing a TV series based on his books?"

"You found all that?" Detective Anthony asked.

Tyrell showed the detectives the files containing the poetry manuscript and the letters. "From the dates on the letters, it looks like he was planning to send them the day after the book launch." Scarr had been murdered before he could mail them.

"Can you print those letters for us?" Uncle Joe asked.

"No problem." While the letters were printing, Tyrell added, "I took a look at the poems."

"And?"

"If you ask me, the guy should have stuck to what he did best."

Of the letters that Tyrell had found on the computer, the one that interested the detectives most was addressed to Andrew Mackie, CEO of Midnight Productions. The detectives paid a visit to Mackie's office in a downtown skyscraper.

Andrew Mackie was a busy man who seemed annoyed to have to speak with them.

"Yeah, we're planning a series based on Scarr's books," he said. "So what? Does that make me a suspect or something?"

"Did Mr. Scarr give you any indication that he was planning to change his mind about the series?" Detective Anthony asked.

"Scarr never gave me any indication of anything," Mackie said. "Except for one meeting, I dealt exclusively with James Afton. The whole thing was his idea. He handled everything with Scarr. I was just waiting for Scarr's signature on the contracts."

"What happens now that he's dead?" Detective Anthony asked.

"What do you mean?"

"I don't think he's going to be signing any contracts."

"Jimmy called me this morning. Scarr's wife is going to sign. We're going to bill it as his final gift to his fans. We can sell this thing worldwide."

"Which means Mrs. Sloane will make a lot of money," Detective Anthony said. "Where does Afton fit in?"

"He's producing. Looks like Jimmy's ship has finally come in."

"Meaning?"

"Meaning Jimmy has made a lot of bad business decisions. From what I hear, he's up to his eyeballs in debt. This deal is going to bail him out. If sales go the way I hope they will, it'll make him a very rich man."

On the way back to the station, the detectives reviewed the case. Dylan Dumont was angry with his father, needed money, and was now going to inherit a million dollars. He had been seen arguing with Scarr the night of the murder. He had no alibi. But could he have got into the locked Belmont Building?

Sara Mystinski didn't have an alibi, either. If Scarr abandoned writing for kids, she would lose a lot of potential money in agent fees. But there was no proof that she knew what Scarr had been planning. And she hadn't been seen arguing with Scarr.

Scarr's wife would gain from her husband's death. She inherited everything except the million dollars he had left his son. But by all accounts, she had seemed happily married. There was nothing that led the detectives to think she had anything to do with her husband's death.

Then there was James Afton. Like Dylan, he had been

seen arguing with Scarr the night of the murder. He had access to the Belmont Building. He stood to lose a lot if Scarr pulled out of the TV deal. But unless the detectives could prove that he knew what Scarr was planning, Afton had no motive. No one had seen him in or near the Belmont that night.

Then someone responded to the police appeal for information. She was James Afton's neighbour. The detectives went to see her.

Valerie Murphy lived directly below Afton on the second floor of a waterfront condominium. She told the detectives that she had been wakened the night of the murder when Afton parked directly under her living room window. As usual, he opened his car door before shutting off his car radio, a bad habit of his that she'd been unable to break, even though she'd asked him a hundred times to be quiet at night. She got up to give him a piece of her mind. But when he got out of his car, he didn't come toward the building. Instead, he crossed the street to the waterfront, where the marina was being expanded. He walked along the dredging site and threw something into the water.

Why had she called the police?

"It didn't look right," she told the detectives. "And when I heard what happened to Mr. Scarr, I thought I should say something. Jim always talked about how Scarr would still be writing bad poetry if it wasn't for him. He said he had talked Scarr into writing horror stories instead, but was getting nothing out of it. Call it intuition, but it made me wonder."

"Do you know what time it was when Mr. Afton

arrived home?" Detective Anthony asked.

"A little after eleven-thirty."

"How do you know?" Uncle Joe asked. It wasn't that he thought she was lying, but Valerie Murphy didn't seem to like James Afton. The timing of events that night was important. He wanted to make sure of every detail of her story.

"*The Tonight Show* was on," she said. "It had just started. Leno was doing his monologue."

Now the detectives were wondering, too. Afton said he had been home by eleven, but *The Tonight Show* started at eleven-thirty. They asked Valerie Murphy to show them where she had been standing when she had seen Afton. From her balcony, she had a good view of the parking lot. She pointed to the parking space, then across the road to the waterfront where a construction crew was hard at work. She told the detectives where Afton had been standing when he threw "something" into the water.

Uncle Joe asked if she had seen what Afton was wearing.

"Sure," she said. "He walked right under the light. He was wearing a light shirt and dark pants."

Uncle Joe looked from the window to where she said she had seen Afton.

"It was a cool night," he said. "Was he wearing anything over his shirt?"

"You mean, like a jacket?" She frowned. "No. I hadn't thought of that. He was wearing it that afternoon. A black leather jacket he paid two thousand dollars for at some chi-chi store in Yorkville a few weeks ago. I know because last week, just after he bought it, he got a little too close to my cigarette in the elevator and freaked out when he thought I had burned a hole in it. He threatened to send me a bill for the whole two thousand."

The detectives thanked the woman. Then they made a call. A couple of hours later, police divers found something almost exactly where Valerie Murphy had said they would. It was a gun.

The detectives were familiar with crime lab guidelines. They knew that evidence found in the water should be kept in water until it could be delivered to the crime lab. They did just that.

The murder weapon

A suspected murder weapon can go through many hands before it reaches the firearms examiner. Usually the police check it for fingerprints. Then a forensic biologist tests it for blood, which can splatter on a gun when it's fired at close range. But because this gun had been found underwater, the procedure was different. It's extremely unlikely that either fingerprints or blood will be found on a gun that has been submerged in water. So the gun went directly to the firearms examiner.

Westcott knew that the gun would begin to rust as soon as he started to dry it. He swabbed the barrel, the breech face, the firing pin and other working areas with preservative so that those areas wouldn't rust.

He confirmed that the gun was a Browning Hi-Power, Model 1935 — as he had already told police.

Then he swabbed out the bore — the inside of the barrel — and tested the swab to see if there was any firearms discharge residue on it. There was. This told Westcott two things — that the gun had been fired since the last time it was cleaned, and that it had not been cleaned before it was thrown into the water.

Next, he tested to see whether this was the gun that had killed Scarr. He worked systematically, following a precise procedure.

First he checked the condition of the gun and all of its safety features.

Then he went to the lab's ammunition locker and found some ammunition with bullets that matched the two types of bullet that had been recovered from Scarr's

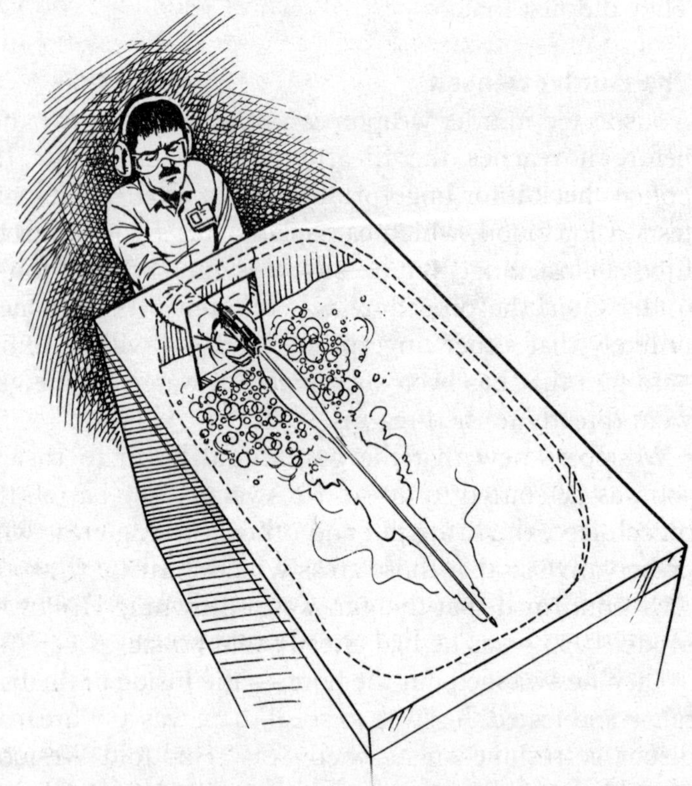

Peter Westcott firing the suspected murder weapon into the water recovery tank

body and from the crime scene. He loaded the first type of ammunition into the suspected murder weapon, put on his safety glasses and his protective ear-wear, and fired into the lab's water recovery tank. This is a big tank of water about ten feet long, three feet wide and four feet deep. When a bullet is fired into water, the water slows down the bullet so quickly that it doesn't hit the bottom or the sides of the tank with enough force to damage any of the markings on it. (Now you know why heroes in action movies often jump into a lake or a river when they're being shot at. After travelling through a couple of feet in water, bullets no longer have enough energy to be lethal.) He fished the bullets out of the tank, reloaded the gun with the second type of ammunition and repeated the process.

Then he tested the gun to see if it could have fired accidentally. He did this by actually dropping the gun and then hitting it with a rawhide mallet. These steps were important because a suspect might claim that the gun had gone off by accident. Westcott wanted to be able to answer questions about this possibility. In this case, the gun did not go off when he hit it or dropped it.

Finally he compared the test bullets to the bullets from the murder weapon. There was no doubt in Westcott's mind that the gun that had been fished from the water was the gun that had been used to kill Edwin Scarr. He recorded his findings and reported them to the police. Then he wrote a detailed report documenting everything he had found.

Uncle Joe and Detective Anthony reviewed the information they had. Afton had been seen arguing with Edwin

Scarr. He stood to lose a great deal if Scarr had backed out of the TV deal, as the letter in Scarr's computer showed he was planning to do. Afton had no solid alibi for the time of the murder. He had claimed he was home by eleven that night, but a neighbour had seen him arrive at his condo after eleven-thirty. He had been seen throwing something into the water. The murder weapon had been found at that exact location.

The detectives went through other material in their files. The photographs from the book launch clearly showed James Afton wearing a black leather jacket. Valerie Murphy had said he was wearing a black leather jacket when he left the condo that day. Witnesses at the book launch had seen him in the jacket. But when Afton had arrived home on that cool night, he had been in his shirtsleeves. What had happened to the jacket?

"You think he got rid of it?" Detective Anthony said.

"A jacket that cost a couple of thousand dollars?" Uncle Joe supposed it was possible. But Afton didn't seem like the kind of person who would get rid of something that expensive. It seemed more likely that he would send it to the cleaners. If he had done that, well, even if there had been anything useful on the jacket, it would be gone now. Still . . .

What about the two drops of blood that had been found on the carpet just outside Afton's office? Had they come from Lorenzo Rego when he'd used the phone in Afton's office? Or had the killer left them there? Had Afton killed Scarr, then gone into his own office for some reason? If so, was there any other evidence in his office? Was there any other blood? Had he left his jacket there? They decided to take a look.

Before they could search Afton's office, the detectives had to apply to a judge for a search warrant. They had to swear that an offence had been committed and that there were reasonable grounds to believe that there was evidence of that offence in Afton's office.

A search warrant does not give the police the right to go on a "fishing expedition." They can search only the place stated on the warrant. They have to say on the warrant what they are looking for — in this case, blood, a jacket and papers or other evidence that might show that Afton knew what Scarr was planning. They would not be allowed to seize anything but these things, unless they discovered illegal items that were used in or obtained as a result of committing a crime.

Despite a thorough search, no more blood was found. Nor did they find anything that showed that Afton knew about Scarr's plans to back out of the TV series. But in the back of Afton's office closet, they found a black leather jacket. The detectives didn't see any blood on it — but blood could be difficult to see on black leather, especially if the blood was fine or the drops were small. They couldn't tell if the jacket had been cleaned recently. They seized it and delivered it to the crime lab.

• • •

"If you ask me, Afton wasn't very smart," I said. "He left two cartridge cases at the scene. He threw away the gun near his house. And he didn't get rid of the jacket."

"You're assuming he did it," Uncle Joe said. "You're also assuming that every murder is carefully planned by a criminal mastermind. The average person doesn't understand how important cartridge cases are. And even if he did it — "

"If?"

"The gun was found at a site where dredging and construction were going on — not a bad drop place. And maybe he had the jacket cleaned before he hung it in the closet. Or maybe there was nothing on it."

"Was there?"

The sun was starting to dip down toward the tops of the pine trees on the other side of the lake. "We'd better get our candles and lanterns ready," Uncle Joe said. "How about I make us some chili for supper?"

"Only if you can cook and talk at the same time," I said.

"I might be able to do that — if I had an extra pair of hands."

I offered him mine. Anything to keep him talking.

CHAPTER 11
Closing In

"WE HAD A MOTIVE for Afton — financial gain," Uncle Joe said. "He had access to the Belmont. He hadn't told the truth about his whereabouts that night. And we found the gun pretty much where he was seen throwing something into the water."

"So you did arrest him?" I said.

Uncle Joe shook his head. "He was seen throwing something. But Valerie Murphy didn't see what he threw. For all we knew, someone else could have thrown that gun into the water before Afton got there."

"Give me a break!" I said.

"We didn't have an eyewitness. No one saw Afton in or around the Belmont that night. There was nothing to tie him definitely to either the weapon or the scene at the time the murder was committed. We needed more."

"Did you get it?"

• • •

The detectives took the jacket to the crime lab. They wanted answers to three questions. Was there any blood on the jacket? If so, was it Scarr's? And was there any evidence that someone had fired a gun while wearing the jacket?

The jacket went first to the lab's chemistry department. The detectives explained what they were looking for. The chemist was skeptical. He asked where the jacket had been since the night of the shooting. Had it been cleaned? Had it been worn? The detectives didn't know. But they guessed that if it hadn't been cleaned, then it had probably hung in Afton's closet the whole time. If that were the case, there was a chance they could find something on it.

The chemist asked if the suspect was right-handed or left-handed.

"Right-handed," Detective Anthony said.

The chemist concentrated on the jacket's right cuff. He dabbed at it with a small aluminum stub that had double-sided adhesive tape on one end. He was looking for gunshot residue.

A cloud of gas is given off when a gun is fired. The gas condenses on whatever it comes into contact with, leaving gunshot residue. This can settle on the gun, the hand of the person firing the gun, that person's sleeve and anything else nearby.

Looked at under a powerful microscope, gunshot residue usually appears as tiny, spherical particles that contain three elements: lead, barium and antimony. By examining the particles dabbed from the jacket, the chemist was able to confirm the presence of gunshot residue. But he cautioned the detectives about what this meant. All that he could say for sure what that the person who had been wearing the jacket had been present when a weapon was fired. It didn't prove that the person had pulled the trigger. There was no way to match gunshot residue to a specific gun. But combined with what the detectives already knew or suspected, it helped.

The jacket went to the biologist next. She examined it under a stereomicroscope and fibre-optic lighting. She angled the light across the surface of the jacket in the same way that Officer Durning had angled his flashlight across the hardwood floor of Scarr's office when he'd looked for footprints. She spotted several small, dull areas on the shiny surface of the leather. She used a test called the Kastle-Meyer to find out if the spots were blood. They were. Now she would do an extraction so that she could generate a DNA profile. She could then see whether this profile matched Scarr's DNA profile. Because the lab was so busy, this could take weeks.

• • •

"You mean you had to wait for weeks?" I asked.

"We didn't have to. At that point, we could have made an arrest."

"Did you?" I asked. "Did you arrest him? Did he confess?"

Uncle Joe just looked at me.

"No, huh?" I said.

"When we searched his office, he hired a lawyer."

"A-ha!" I said. "That meant he had something to hide."

"Not necessarily," Uncle Joe said. "The truth is, most people get nervous when the police start poking around. They start thinking about Donald Marshall and Hurricane Carter."

"Innocent people who ended up in prison," I said.

"Right," Uncle Joe said. "It really doesn't tell you anything when a suspect contacts a lawyer to find out what's going on and what their rights are. I'd probably do the same thing myself. Afton hired Michael Stott, a criminal defence lawyer."

"Do you know him?"

"Very well."

• • •

If Afton worried that hiring a lawyer would make him look guilty, he wasn't alone, Uncle Joe said. Most people who contact a criminal lawyer share that worry. Stott usually tells his clients that if the police have executed a search warrant, then they're already suspicious. Hiring a lawyer wouldn't hurt and would definitely help.

At his first meeting with a client, Stott always asks a lot of questions and listens carefully to the answers. He tries to form a good picture of the person under police suspicion. He also wants to know everything the police have already asked and everything his client has told them.

He tells clients that the most powerful right a citizen has is the right to remain silent. Most people are nervous when police want to question them. Often they aren't sure what the police are looking for or why they're asking certain questions. Because of this, they may not express themselves clearly. They may say things that can be taken out of context and even used against them later. Stott always reminds clients that they are presumed innocent until proven guilty and explains the concept of lawyer-client privilege. He warns that if they are arrested, they should contact him immediately and refuse to answer any questions.

The detectives were sure Afton was their man and felt they had enough evidence to get an arrest warrant. But they knew their case was circumstantial. They wanted to make it as strong as possible.

They were sure they weren't going to find anyone who had seen Afton pull the trigger. But there was still a chance they could prove that Afton had entered or was near the Belmont Building that night.

They turned to the security videotapes that they had collected from various stores and buildings during the canvass. Many were of poor quality. Some were completely useless. But one turned out to be helpful. The security camera at a gas station around the corner from the Belmont clearly showed James Afton making a credit-card payment at the cash at 10:45 on the night of the murder.

The detectives paid a visit to the gas station, talked to the manager and had him retrieve a copy of Afton's credit-card slip. It confirmed what the video had told them. James Afton had filled up the tank of his leased car a block from the Belmont Building at 10:45 — an hour after Lorenzo Rego had seen Edwin Scarr in the elevator, and eighteen minutes before someone had pulled the plug on Scarr's computer. That — together with the gun, the witness who had seen Afton dispose of the gun, the leather jacket, and the financial motive — made James Afton seem like a good enough suspect to arrest. The detectives applied for an arrest warrant.

• • •

"Finally," I said. "You nailed him."

"We arrested him," Uncle Joe said. The way he said it made me think he wasn't agreeing with me.

"But you had all the evidence you needed," I said. Then, "Didn't you?"

All of a sudden, a light came on in the kitchen.

"Looks like we're back in business," Uncle Joe said. "Now all we need is a snow plow."

I didn't care about the lights or the plow.

"Come on, Uncle Joe. You nailed him, right?"

DO YOU KNOW YOUR RIGHTS?[9]

Under the Canadian Charter of Rights and Freedoms, Canadians are guaranteed certain legal rights when they are arrested. These include:

- The right to remain silent when questioned by the police.
- The right to be told why you have been arrested or detained.
- The right to be told that you can hire and instruct a lawyer.
- The right to be told about the availability of duty counsel (defence lawyers paid by the government) and legal aid.
- The right to speak to a lawyer in private as soon as possible.
- The right to a trial in a reasonable period of time.
- The right to be presumed innocent until proved guilty.
- The right to be released on bail unless there is a good reason to be kept in custody.
- The right to refuse to testify at your own trial.

IS THE EVIDENCE DIRECT OR CIRCUMSTANTIAL?[10]

There are two kinds of evidence:

Direct evidence is evidence given by witnesses who actually saw a crime being committed. For example, Mr. Black testifies that he saw Mr. Pink shoot Mr. Green.

Circumstantial evidence is evidence that tends to incriminate someone — although other conclusions could be drawn from it. For example, Mr. Black testifies that he saw Mr. Pink running from the house where Mr. Green has just been shot dead. From this, one might conclude that Mr. Pink shot Mr. Green. But the same fact could let the defence argue that Mr. Pink fled because he was afraid that he, too, would be shot.

CHAPTER 12
Enter the Lawyers

"DON'T TELL ME, let me guess," Uncle Joe said. "You think that it was pretty much case closed after that. When confronted with everything we had, Afton broke down and confessed, right?"

Okay, so maybe I had been thinking that. Obviously, I was wrong.

"The case wasn't over," Uncle Joe said. "Not by a long shot. It was another year before things got settled."

"A year?" I stared at my uncle. "What happened? Did he take off before you could arrest him?"

"Nope. He was at home when we arrested him."

"So what took so long?"

"Due process."

• • •

Uncle Joe and Detective Anthony went to Afton's condo with a warrant and informed him that he was under arrest. They told him that he had "the right to retain and instruct legal counsel without delay." He had the right to telephone any lawyer that he wished and, if he needed it, to get free advice from a legal aid lawyer. They asked him, "Do you understand? Do you wish to telephone a lawyer now?'

Afton said he did. After a brief conversation, he called Uncle Joe to the phone. Michael Stott was on the line. In response to his questions, Uncle Joe told the lawyer that

Afton had been charged and confirmed that he had been read his right to counsel. Stott informed Uncle Joe that Afton was declining to answer any questions for now. Then he asked to speak with Afton again.

People often think that the police have to stop asking questions after an accused has contacted his lawyer. They also think that the accused can't be questioned without his lawyer present. Neither is true. The accused has a right to contact a lawyer. After he has done that, the police can still ask questions. If the accused has listened to his lawyer, he might tell police, "On the advice of counsel, I don't wish to discuss it at this time." But often people don't respond that way. Many of them talk, even after their lawyers have warned them not to. Some criminal defence lawyers say that their clients are often their own worst enemies.

After Afton was arrested, he was taken to the police station where he was fingerprinted, photographed, weighed and measured. He seemed upset, but he took his lawyer's advice. When the police started to ask him more questions, he chose not to answer.

Soon after they made the arrest, the detectives alerted the head Crown attorney for the area.

• • •

"The Crown attorney is your lawyer, right?" I asked Uncle Joe.

Uncle Joe shook his head. "Crown attorneys aren't police lawyers, they're government lawyers," he said. "It's their job to decide if there's enough evidence to take a case to trial. If there is, they prosecute the case."

"So you must have been talking to them all along," I said.

That earned me another shake of Uncle Joe's head.

"Crown attorneys don't work the way district attorneys do in the U.S.," he said. "In the majority of cases, the Crown attorney doesn't get involved until after we've made an arrest. Then we meet with the head Crown and give him a rundown of the case. He assigns a Crown attorney to the case."

• • •

Because the case was circumstantial, the head Crown assigned someone with a lot of experience prosecuting murder trials.

The first thing Crown attorney Maria Wesolowski always does is contact the accused's lawyer. She told Stott that he would get full disclosure of the evidence as it became available. In other words, the defence would get all of the information relating to the case — copies of police reports, statements from witnesses, copies of the reports from the crime lab. Some things would take time. The police were still waiting for some of the DNA evidence. Some videotaped statements still had to be transcribed.

Some people think it isn't fair that Crown attorneys have to tell the defence everything they know, while the defence doesn't have to tell the Crown anything. But in Canada, a person is presumed innocent until he is proved guilty. It's up to the Crown to prove guilt "beyond a reasonable doubt." To defend himself, a person needs to know the details of the charges against him. Usually by the time a person is arrested, the police have used the full power of the law to build their case. They've had access to many resources. So has the government, which assigns a Crown attorney to prosecute the case. An individual citizen doesn't have the same power and resources.

Before 1991, there were different views on how much information the Crown had to disclose to the defence and when they had to do it. A Supreme Court of Canada decision case changed that. In its Stinchcombe decision, the Supreme Court said that the evidence gathered by the police belongs not to the Crown, but to the public, and that it should be used to see that justice is done.[11] This doesn't always mean convicting a person. Often justice is done when a person is found not guilty. The Stinchcombe decision said that the Crown must disclose all of the information relevant to a case, whether the Crown plans to use the information or not, and whether the information supports the Crown case or the defence case. It also said that the Crown must disclose its evidence before the accused makes a plea. A person shouldn't have to plead to a charge without knowing all of the facts.

Bail

Under Canada's Criminal Code, someone arrested for an offense and held in custody must have a bail hearing within twenty-four hours of arrest. This is also called a "show cause" hearing because generally it is up to the Crown to show cause why the accused should be kept in custody. But when a person is charged with murder, there is no automatic bail hearing. Instead, it's up to the accused to apply for bail and to show why he should be released.

Stott's first priority was to try to get his client out on bail. Wesolowski was determined to keep him in custody until the trial.

Judges consider a number of things when deciding whether to grant bail to someone accused of murder. The first is how likely it is that the person will show up for trial. If the Crown can make a good case that the person will flee or go into hiding, the person will not get bail. Second is the matter of public safety — is there a danger that the person will commit another crime if he is released? If the person has a criminal record, that will be considered, too. Finally, the judge considers how granting bail will affect the public's confidence in the administration of justice. People usually have more confidence when an accused murderer is kept in custody until his case is heard. The judge also considers how serious the crime is and how strong the Crown's case is.

The accused's lawyer can apply for a bail hearing on three days' notice. But because the charge against Afton was so serious, Stott did not rush. He wanted his client to have the best possible chance of being free until his trial. That meant finding people in the community who would agree to speak on his behalf. It also meant arranging a surety for Afton.

In the United States, a person can get out on bail by paying a large amount of money (which they lose if they don't appear for trial), or by paying a fee to a bail bondsman who puts up the money. In Canada, it's different. In Canada, the court can ask for a surety. A surety is a person who vouches for the accused and pledges a sum of money to guarantee that the accused will show up for trial. The amount is far less than the million-dollar bails shown on American television. If the accused doesn't show up for trial, the surety may lose the money he or she has pledged. This gives the surety an interest in keeping an eye on the accused.

James Afton's sister, a nurse at a children's hospital, agreed to act as a surety. Stott also gathered affidavits — legal statements to use in court — from people who knew Afton, had done business with him and were willing to stand up for him. Two weeks after he was arrested, James Afton had his bail hearing.

The Crown opposed Afton's release. At the hearing, Wesolowski called Uncle Joe to explain the evidence he would give at trial. He outlined what he had discovered in his investigation. He talked about Afton's motive and the fact that Afton had lied about his whereabouts that night. He said that Afton had been seen disposing of the murder weapon, and that blood and gunshot residue had been found on his jacket.

Stott argued that there was no evidence that his client had been in the Belmont Building that night. He said that Afton had been seen throwing something into the water, but that the witness had not been able to tell police what he had thrown. He said that until a DNA analysis had been done, there was no evidence that the blood on Afton's jacket was the victim's blood. The gunshot residue, he said, proved nothing.

Stott called on Afton's sister, who said that her brother had had many business problems, but that he had never been in any real trouble. She said that Afton and the victim had been best friends. Stott presented the affidavits from Afton's other friends and associates. These also vouched for Afton.

Wesolowski cross-examined Afton's sister. She wanted to understand what kind of woman she was. She also wanted Afton's sister to understand the seriousness of what she was doing. Did she realize what was at stake? Was she willing to risk losing her house if her brother didn't show up for his trial? Was she prepared to be responsible for him?

In the end, the judge granted bail. Afton had no criminal record. He had roots in the community. His surety seemed reputable and reliable. There was little likelihood that Afton would commit another crime if released. And although the police had gathered a lot of evidence, it was circumstantial. There were no eyewitnesses.

Afton had to agree to a number of bail conditions. He was not allowed to travel outside of Ontario. He had to surrender his passport. He had to report to the police every week. He was not allowed to have any firearms or ammunition. And he had to agree not to communicate with any witnesses who would be called by the Crown. This included Valerie Murphy, who said she had seen him dispose of the gun, Andrew Mackie, with whom he was doing business, and Jennifer Sloane, Scarr's widow.

CHAPTER 13

The Wheels of Justice Start to Turn

"SO, TWO WEEKS after James Afton was arrested, he was out on bail. Then what?" I said. "You said it was months before the case was over. Did he skip bail?"

"No," Uncle Joe said. "He was released. He went to live with his sister. He continued on with his life, although I guess he was under a lot of stress. And I continued on with mine. I got a couple more cases. I — "

"But what about this case? What was going on?"

"After Afton was released on bail, a date was set for a preliminary inquiry."

"A what?"

"A hearing before a judge in which the Crown has to show that there is enough evidence to send the case to trial. If there isn't enough evidence, the charges are dropped. If there is, the judge sets a trial date."

• • •

The lawyers on both sides estimated that they would need at least two weeks for the preliminary inquiry. A date was set for five months after Afton's arrest. In an overburdened criminal justice system, things take time.

In the meantime, both lawyers prepared.

Maria Wesolowski interviewed all of the witnesses in the case. She was careful never to meet with them alone. Uncle Joe or Detective Anthony was always with her. She didn't want the defence to accuse her of influencing witnesses.

She explained the court process to each witness. Unlike the "professional witnesses" she would call — the police officers and the forensic experts — none of these people had testified in court before. She wanted them to be prepared for what they would face. Before she asked any questions, she told each witness three things.

First, she reminded them to tell their story in their own way. "Don't let anyone put words in your mouth about what you remember," she said. "And that includes me." Second, she said, "If you're certain of something, don't let anyone change your mind. If you're sure something happened at ten o'clock, don't let someone suggest to you that it happened at nine or at eleven." Third, she told them never to guess. "If you're not sure, say you're not sure. Your duty is to tell what you honestly saw and heard."

Then she went through what each witness had said to the police and what they remembered. She asked Lorenzo Rego when he last saw Edwin Scarr alive, how he had discovered the body and what he had done immediately afterwards. She asked how he could be certain about the time he had seen Scarr in the elevator. She told him that if he had any doubts, he should say so. But Rego was sure.

She interviewed Trevor Henson, Sara Mystinski and Anna Farrow. Their knowledge of the changes Scarr was planning to make could help establish motive. She spoke to previous business associates of Afton's, whose knowledge of his business problems and debt could also help with motive. She spoke to Andrew Mackie, who explained how much money Afton would have lost if Scarr had backed out of the TV deal — and how much he could make now that Scarr was dead. She interviewed the two people who had seen Afton and Scarr arguing at the bookstore.

Several of the witnesses who had known Scarr for a long time could also testify that he owned an unregistered firearm, that he kept it in his office and that Afton knew about it. This would link the weapon to both the victim and the accused.

She interviewed Valerie Murphy, who had seen Afton throw something into the water the night of the murder. This witness posed a problem. She had told police that Afton had returned home a little after eleven-thirty that night, but now she wasn't positive of the time. She had been napping when she heard his car. It had been dark. She had gone to the balcony to complain about the noise, but he had walked away. After watching him cross the street and throw something into the water, she got tired of waiting and lay down again. She had told police that *The Tonight Show* was on when he woke her up. But now she wasn't sure if she had seen the beginning, middle or end of the show. Still, she was pretty sure she had seen Afton a little after eleven-thirty. And she had definitely seen him throw something into the water.

Wesolowski asked Detective Anthony, who was with her at the time, to make a note of this. This would have to be disclosed to the defence.

While she waited for the preliminary hearing, Wesolowski also reviewed the evidence that would be presented by forensic scientists and police officers.

Uncle Joe was certain that Michael Stott was busy, too. He would have interviewed Afton about what had happened the night of the murder and quizzed him about some of the problem areas. The jacket was critical to the case, and Stott would want to know everything he could about it.

• • •

"Would he even believe Afton's story?" I asked. "It seems pretty weak."

"Stott has been a criminal lawyer for a long time," Uncle Joe said. "He knows you have to keep an open mind. When you're a lawyer — and when you're a detective — people tell you a lot of strange things. Often it turns out that they're telling the truth."

• • •

Stott works hard for his clients, Uncle Joe said. He's been careful throughout his career to develop a respectful relationship with the Crown attorneys and with the police. Some Crowns think defence lawyers defend "scum." Some defence lawyers think Crowns act as if they're police lawyers. Some police officers don't trust defence lawyers. Stott understands this. But he knows that experienced homicide investigators are a good source of information, so he's careful not to burn bridges — although this has never stopped him from grilling police officers on the witness stand, when he has to.

Stott went through the boxes of material that the Homicide Squad had assembled on Afton. He read all of the police notes, and went through all of the statements that were available. Some hadn't been transcribed yet. He would have to wait for those. Like the Crown, he would also have to wait for the results of some of the forensic evidence.

Knowing Stott, Uncle Joe said, he also visited the Belmont Building to see for himself what it looked like.

He would have walked through the whole suite of offices and checked the layout, Afton's office and the office where Scarr's body had been found. From what would happen later, Uncle Joe also knew that Stott had checked out the gas station where Afton had filled up his tank. He must have stood near the cash, watched cars pull in and fill up, then watched drivers come in, pay for their gas and then drive off again. He also visited Afton's condo to see for himself what Valerie Murphy might have seen. He walked across the road to the waterfront, then looked back at the building again, focusing in on the neighbour's windows.

With his client's approval, he hired his own experts to examine the jacket and review the crime lab's findings. He also engaged a private investigator on Afton's behalf to find out what he could from witnesses and to try to dig up new information. As the police had done, the investigator looked carefully into Scarr's life to find out who else may have wanted to kill him.

Days dragged by and turned into weeks. Weeks turned into months. While James Afton waited for his preliminary inquiry, he tried to carry on with his life. That's never easy for an accused, Uncle Joe said. He probably worried that some of his friends believed he'd killed Scarr. (If people he knew were ready to believe the worst, what would twelve strangers on a jury think?)

The only bright spot in his life was that the TV deal was still on. Jennifer Sloane was proud of her late husband's books and thought the TV project was a great idea. She had signed the papers before Afton was arrested. But the production was moving forward without

Afton. He wasn't allowed to contact Andrew Mackie. But he would eventually make money from the deal. And he was going to need it. Michael Stott was one of the best criminal lawyers in the city. That meant he didn't come cheap.

The preliminary inquiry

Finally, it was time for the preliminary inquiry. At a preliminary inquiry, the Crown doesn't have to present its full case. It only has to bring enough evidence to convince the judge that a reasonable jury, properly instructed, could convict. The important word is "could." The Crown does not have to show that a jury would convict.

The preliminary inquiry is held in front of a judge. There is no jury.

Everything witnesses say is recorded. Both sides get transcripts afterwards. These can be important. Sometimes witnesses change their stories between the preliminary inquiry and the trial. Sometimes witnesses disappear. Sometimes they become ill and are unable to testify at trial. Sometimes they die. In all of these cases, testimony from the preliminary inquiry can be used at the trial.

Wesolowski called her witnesses. She called one of the homicide detectives. She presented evidence from the firearms examiner, the forensic biologist and the forensic chemist. She called the cleaner who had found the body, the bookstore employee who had seen Afton and Scarr argue, the gas station manager and Valerie Murphy, who had seen him throw something in the water.

In presenting her case, Wesolowski concentrated on showing that there was more than enough evidence to take the case to trial. The forensic evidence was particularly important. In murder cases, victims could not tell their side of the story. Forensic evidence allowed the dead to speak.

Michael Stott listened closely. The preliminary inquiry would give him a good understanding of the Crown's case. It was also his first chance to question some of the witnesses. Crown witnesses are free to speak with the defence outside of the courtroom, but they don't have to. Some of them, like Valerie Murphy, had chosen not to. Stott had read all of the witness statements, but these only told him so much. "It's not the same when the puck hits the ice and they take the stand," he often said. The preliminary inquiry would let him evaluate each witness and the weight they might carry at trial.

When Stott cross-examined these witnesses, he didn't have to worry about the reactions of twelve ordinary citizens on a jury. He could concentrate on digging into the Crown's evidence and learning the strengths and weaknesses of its case. But he was also cautious. He wanted to find out as much as he could without giving the Crown too many clues about the defence that he would present if the case went to trial.

The preliminary inquiry took two weeks. The judge's decision was no surprise. There was enough evidence to proceed to trial. A date was set. The trial of James Afton for the murder of Edwin Sloane, a.k.a. Edwin Scarr, would take place in five months.

• • •

"But that's almost a year from the time Edwin Scarr was murdered!"

"That's right," Uncle Joe said. "Like I said, things take

time. For people on the outside, it may seem to take too long. But for everyone involved, time seems to fly. There's so much to do to prepare for the trial."

Chapter 14

The Accused's Day in Court

"FINALLY — " Uncle Joe began.

"The trial started," I finished for him.

Uncle Joe smiled. "First there was a pre-trial conference."

"A what?"

"A meeting between the two lawyers and the judge."

"Why did they have to meet again? Didn't they just see each other at the preliminary hearing."

"A trial is time-consuming — and expensive," Uncle Joe said. "Think of what you need. A courtroom and courtroom staff. A judge to preside over the trial. A Crown attorney to prosecute the case and a defence lawyer to defend. The homicide detectives who investigated the case have to attend the trial. You need twelve jurors, all of whom have busy lives. They may have to take time off work or find someone to look after their children. Then there are all the witnesses who have to come to court and testify. Some of them may have to sit around and wait. The best the lawyers can do is estimate when witnesses will take the stand. They can't always predict how long each witness will testify — a lot depends on how their testimony goes, how important it is, and how many questions the other side asks in cross-examination. It all adds up to a lot of people, a lot of time and a lot of money."

• • •

Pre-trial conferences are usually held about six weeks before a trial. Both lawyers meet with the judge, who usually asks what penalty the Crown will seek. In this case, the Crown contended that James Afton had gone to Scarr's office with the intention of killing him, to prevent him from backing out of the TV deal. The Crown believed it was a planned and deliberate act: first-degree murder. This carried a mandatory life sentence, with no chance of parole for twenty-five years.

The judge asked if the case could be settled without going to trial. Sometimes, if the Crown feels its case is strong in proving intentional murder, but weak in proving that it was planned and deliberate, it might offer the accused a chance to plead guilty to second-degree murder and forego a trial. This conviction also carries a life sentence, but allows for earlier parole. In this case, however, Wesolowksi made no such offer.

The judge also asked if the defence had received all the information it needed from the Crown. Stott had had to wrangle with the Crown's office over the past few months to make sure he had everything. Now he believed he did, and he told the judge so.

Finally, it was time for the trial.

Before the jury is chosen, the judge and the lawyers often discuss technical business. For example, sometimes the defence wants to change the location of the trial. This happens when the case has received so much publicity that the defence is afraid it will be impossible to find jurors who haven't already made up their minds. Sometimes the defence argues that the police did not get the proper search warrants, or that their client's rights under the Canadian Charter of Rights and Freedoms haven't been respected. Sometimes the lawyers discuss how the jury will be chosen.

The jury

The twelve men and women who sit on a jury in a criminal case are called the "triers of fact." It is up to them to listen to the facts and decide whether a person has been proved guilty "beyond a reasonable doubt."

All citizens must report for jury duty when they are called. Every province has its own laws about who is eligible to serve on a jury and how each is chosen.

In some countries, like the United States, the prosecution and the defence can ask a lot of questions to people who are called for jury duty. Some defence lawyers hire jury experts to research what different groups of people generally think about the case. The defence uses this information to try to select a jury favourable to its client.

In Canada, the judicial system guarantees people an impartial jury, not a favourable one. For this reason, lawyers are not allowed to investigate jurors. Instead, they're given the name, occupation and address of each person summoned for jury duty. As each one comes forward, the lawyers can also see roughly how old the person is. But in most cases, that's all the information they get.

Potential jurors are asked to look at the accused and to state their name and occupation. In a murder case, the lawyer on each side has the right to reject twenty prospective jurors without giving any reason. This is called a peremptory challenge. In some cases, jurors can be "challenged for cause." For example, if the case is controversial or if the accused is a member of a visible minority, a lawyer may worry that people will be influenced by what they have heard or who the accused is. In these cases, the judge may allow jurors to be asked about this. The question has to be approved by the judge. If a question like this is allowed, there is no limit to the number of jurors who may be rejected based on their answer.

Depending on their position in a case, lawyers often have specific ideas about who they want on a jury. A prosecutor might want to reject nurses and social workers, because these are people who tend to want to help others and be forgiving. A defence lawyer might want people who are a little "rough around the edges," thinking they may be more sympathetic to the accused. A lawyer defending a fraud case might not want a bank manager on the jury. A prosecutor might reject engineers and architects, because people in these occupations like everything to be exact — they may need positive proof before they will pronounce an accused guilty. Under the law, one-hundred-percent proof isn't required. Most lawyers watch jurors' body language. If prospective jurors won't look at the accused, it could be because they're already assuming guilt. Sometimes lawyers are guided by intuition — they just "get a vibe."

As each juror was chosen in James Afton's case, he or she was sworn in. It took a full morning to select the jury. In some cases, jury selection takes longer.

The trial begins

First the charge was read for the accused, and he was asked for his plea.

"Not guilty."

Then the judge made some introductory remarks. She explained to the jurors how the trial would operate, reminded them not to discuss the case with anyone and told them to keep an open mind.

The defence asked for witnesses to be kept from the courtroom until it was their turn to give evidence. This was important because the witnesses would be asked to tell what they personally knew about the facts of the case. They had to be able to do this without being influenced by the testimony of others. The investigating officers and forensic experts were excluded from this request.

Then the Crown attorney was asked to give her opening statement. Maria Wesolowski turned her attention to the jury. For the rest of the trial, she would closely watch the twelve men and women in the jury box. She would try to gauge their reaction to witnesses and to the defence. She would also try to make sure that they understood everything that was being said. This would be especially important when it came to the forensic evidence. Explanations would have to be clear so that they could understand what each piece of evidence meant and how important it was to the case.

In her opening statement, Wesolowski summarized the evidence that she would present and outlined her theory of the case. Crown attorneys are not allowed to make an argument in their opening. They are not allowed to say, "This man is guilty, and here's why." She concentrated on making sure that the jurors had a good idea why they were there, what the case was about and what they could generally expect to happen.

She chose her words carefully. She knew that it was important not to make too many promises about what the jury would hear. She didn't want to give the defence a chance to say at the end of the trial, "Ms. Wesolowski said you were going to hear such-and-such. But you didn't hear that, did you?" This could make the jury wonder why she hadn't lived up to her promise.

In the vast majority of cases, the defence does not make an opening statement immediately. Sometimes, though, if they're sure how the case will develop, defence lawyers ask the judge if they can "open" right after the Crown. Then, as the jurors listen to the Crown's full case, they already have some idea of the defence's view of events. In this case, though, Stott did not make an opening statement at this point.

Witnesses

As witnesses are called to testify, they are asked to take an oath or to "affirm" (promise) that they will tell the truth. Lying under oath, called perjury, is a criminal offence.

There are two kinds of witnesses. Non-expert witnesses are people who know something about the crime itself or about the circumstances surrounding the crime. They can answer questions only about what they personally saw or heard and know to be true. They're generally not allowed to give "hearsay" evidence (evidence that is based on what someone else has told them), although there are exceptions. For example, they can say what the accused told them. They're not allowed to give opinions, but must stick to the facts.

Expert witnesses are people who are qualified in their professions and who are allowed to offer professional opinions. They have to demonstrate at each trial that they are experts. In many cases, one side or the other disputes this. The judge decides if someone is an expert. In Afton's case, the expert witnesses included the forensic scientists who examined much of the evidence from this case.

CHAPTER 15
The Crown's Case

"NOW?" I said.

"Now what?"

"Now James Afton gets nailed for the murder of Edwin Scarr?"

"You think that's going to happen?" Uncle Joe said.

"Isn't it?"

"When a case is circumstantial, you can never be sure of anything," he said. "But the Crown was prepared."

• • •

The Crown presents its case first. Its examination of witnesses is called the examination-in-chief. After the Crown has finished questioning each witness, the defence is allowed to cross-examine.

Before the trial, Wesolowski had met with each witness again. She gave each one a copy of their preliminary inquiry testimony and asked them to read over what they had said. If they remembered things differently now, she wanted to know. She told them that the transcripts would refresh their memories, but cautioned them not to memorize them.

The defence also had copies of the transcripts. Stott would be listening for any differences between what witnesses had said at the preliminary inquiry and what they said now. Wesolowski knew that some things that some witnesses would say at the trial would not exactly match what they had said at the preliminary inquiry. This was normal. By now, nearly a year had passed since Edwin Scarr had been murdered. But if there were too many differences, or the differences were too big, the jury might think a witness was unreliable or that the testimony should not be believed.

In preparing her case, Wesolowski thought about the order of the witnesses. She liked to start strong and end strong. If there were any weak elements to her case, she put those in the middle. She was also mindful of one important fact in any murder trial: the accused was in the courtroom, but the victim was not. "The victim can get lost very quickly," she often said. The jury would hear all about the accused, but unless Wesolowski kept reminding them, they might forget about the victim. She would paint a picture of the deceased and remind jurors that Edwin Sloane (as he would be referred to throughout the trial) was a much-loved children's writer, that he was recently married, that he had been planning a long and successful career.

As Stott listened to the Crown's case unfold, he would be thinking about his strategy for cross-examining each witness. His job was to bring out any evidence that could help his client. He would point out where Crown evidence was weak, or where there might be another explanation for a witness's testimony. If he could present an alternative scenario that addressed all of the facts, but also showed that they did not necessarily prove his client was a murderer, then he could create "reasonable doubt" in the jurors' minds.

Witness: Andrew Mackie

Wesolowski started by presenting evidence that showed that James Afton had a powerful motive for murder: greed. She called Andrew Mackie, who told the court about the TV-production deal that was worth millions of dollars and that would make James Afton rich.

Stott cross-examined Mackie. He asked if Mackie had known that Sloane was going to pull out of the deal. Mackie said he had not. He asked if Mackie would have been angry if Sloane had pulled out at the last minute. Mackie said that he would have been. He asked if Mackie also stood to make a lot of money on the deal. Mackie said that he did. Then Stott asked, "Would you have killed Mr. Sloane if he had threatened to pull out?"

"No," Mackie said, "I most certainly would not."

As he went to sit down again, Stott turned to Mackie.

"Do you own a cottage?"

"Yes," Mackie said. He owned a place up north.

"Did Mr. Afton and Mr. Sloane visit you at that cottage?"

"Yes," Mackie said. "They did."

"When?" Stott asked.

"In early March last year." Mackie said he remembered because he was up at the cottage with his kids for March break.

Both Wesolowski and Uncle Joe wondered why Stott had asked these last few questions.

Witnesses: other business associates

Wesolowski called previous associates of Afton's, who testified about Afton's past business problems and his large debt. Then Stott asked these witnesses if they had they ever known Afton to commit a crime as a result of business difficulties. They all said no. Had they known him to commit a violent act? They had not. Had they known him to commit murder? They had not.

Witness: Sara Mystinski

Wesolowski called Sara Mystinksi, the victim's agent, who said she had last seen Sloane at the book launch and that he had been in a good mood. She told the court when Sloane had left the launch and when Afton had left.

In his cross-examination, Stott asked if Afton had told her where he was going.

"He said he was going home."

"Did he say or do anything to give you the idea he was upset with Mr. Sloane?"

"No."

"Did you know that Mr. Sloane was planning to quit writing for children?"

"No, I didn't."

"Wasn't that strange? After all, you were his agent."

"Edwin could be very secretive."

"Did my client say or do anything that made you think that he knew about the changes Mr. Sloane was planning?"

"No, he didn't."

"So it was possible that no one knew except Mr. Sloane himself, isn't it?"

"Yes, I suppose."

Stott paused a moment, then asked, "Isn't it true that as Mr. Sloane's agent, you would have lost a great deal if he had stopped writing children's books?"

"Yes," she said, "I suppose so."

Witness: the bookstore employee

The employee testified about seeing the victim and the accused in a heated argument. Under cross-examination, she admitted that she hadn't heard what they were arguing about. Yes, she said, it could have been over almost anything.

Witness: Detective Joe Morrison

Wesolowski then moved to the circumstances surrounding Sloane's death. She called Uncle Joe, who testified about the investigation. He said that Sloane had been found in his office and that Afton had an office in the same suite. He introduced the videotape and the credit-card transaction slip that showed that Afton had bought gas only one block away from the Belmont Building, at 10:45 on the night of the murder. He told the jurors that the Belmont was not on Afton's direct route home from the bookstore. He explained where the police had found the murder weapon and the jacket.

Michael Stott stood up.

"Did you take steps to check how many people went in and out of the Belmont Building after it was locked at six o'clock the night of the murder?"

"Yes," the detective said, "we did."

"What did you discover?"

"Two people had signed the log at the security desk."

"Was either of those people James Afton?"

"No."

"Does everyone who works here have to sign in?"

The detective explained that people who worked in the Belmont had security codes and can get in and out without passing security.

"Did you check which codes have been punched in?" Stott asked.

"No."

"Why not?"

"There's no way to check. The security system at the Belmont is too old."

"Approximately how many people work in the Belmont Building?"

"Over three hundred."

Stott asked if the police could account for the whereabouts of each and every one of those people that night.

"No."

"In other words, you don't know for sure who else was in the building that night?"

Uncle Joe had to admit this was true.

Stott then asked about the videotape. "It showed that Sloane had been in the area, but not in the Belmont, correct?" Correct, Uncle Joe said.

Then Stott asked about Sloane's son. Wasn't it true that Dylan Dumont had been seen arguing with his father? Wasn't it true that he had said he resented his father's wealth? Wasn't it true that he wanted money from Sloane for his university education? Wasn't it true that he inherited a million dollars in Sloane's will? Wasn't it true that he had no alibi for the time of the murder?

Uncle Joe had to admit that it was all true.

Stott asked how long it took to drive from the Belmont Building to James Afton's condo.

"At that time of night, about fifteen minutes," Uncle Joe said. From the look on Stott's face, Uncle Joe knew that he was confirming what the lawyer already knew.

Witness: the gas station manager

Wesolowski called the gas station manager to the stand. He testified that James Afton had come in to the station that night to buy gas. He identified the credit-card slip for the purchase and told the court the time at which the purchase had been made — 10:45 PM, only eighteen minutes before the cord was yanked from Edwin Sloane's computer.

Under cross-examination by Stott, the manager explained where the gas station was in relation to the Belmont Building. He agreed that Afton was a regular customer. He also agreed that Afton had once told him that he often drove out of his way to buy gas there because the prices were usually lower than at gas stations on the other side of town, where Afton lived. Stott asked if he had seen in which direction Afton's car had gone when he left the gas station.

"No, I didn't."

"Did you see which direction Mr. Afton came from?"

"No."

"So, it's possible that Mr. Afton arrived and left again without passing by the Belmont Building, isn't it?"

"Yes," the manager said. "It's possible."

Witness: Valerie Murphy

Valerie Murphy was called. Wesolowski didn't ask her what time it was when she had seen Afton return home. Murphy's memory on that point was too shaky. Instead, she focused on what Murphy had seen after Afton returned home: Afton throwing something into the water. Did Murphy know what the police had found at that spot?

Yes, she said. A gun.

Stott began his cross-examination by asking how long Murphy had known Afton, and under what circumstances she had spoken with him in the past. He got her to talk about how Afton had woken her up out of a sound sleep. Murphy agreed that it had annoyed her. Stott asked if she had complained about Afton to the condo committee. He knew about this from Afton and from his own private investigator. She gave the answer Stott knew she would: yes, she had complained.

"You don't like Mr. Afton very much, do you?" Stott asked.

"No, I don't. But — "

Stott then asked her about the night of the murder. It had been dark. She had been roused from a sound sleep. The water was far away. How could she have seen what Afton had thrown into the water?

She admitted that she hadn't actually seen the object.

"For all you knew, it could have been a rock. Isn't that right?" Stott said.

"Yes," Murphy said. "But the police found — "

Then Stott zeroed in on time. He knew that Valerie Murphy wasn't positive about exactly when she had seen Afton return home. Since that could be important for his case, he questioned her about it. She had told the police that the first thing she did when she woke up was shut off the TV, was that right? She said it was. He asked her what time that was. At first she said eleven-thirty. But under questioning, she admitted that it could have been later than that, but that Afton had definitely woken her up during *The Tonight Show*. Then she admitted that she wasn't sure when she had dozed off. She became flustered at all of the questions on this one small point. She said she thought she had dozed off during her favourite sitcom, then she admitted that it was hard to be positive because she had "sort of faded in and out all night."

"So you're not sure exactly when you fell asleep?"

"No, but — "

"And you're not sure exactly when you woke up?"

"No."

"And you're not sure what was on TV when you fell asleep?"

"Well, no."

"You faded in and out and saw a lot of different shows on TV that night?"

"Yes, but — "

"And the first thing you did when Mr. Afton arrived home was shut off the TV?"

"Yes."

"Did you turn it on again later?"

"No."

"So, really, with all that fading in and out, it's hard to be positive about what was on TV when Mr. Afton arrived home, isn't it?"

She had to admit that it was. But, she said, it didn't change what she had seen.

Witness: Officer Durning

Having addressed Afton's motive and opportunity to commit the murder, Wesolowski turned to the forensic evidence. She called the Identification officer, who presented a sketch of the crime scene. He then showed photographs and testified about the evidence that had been collected — the cartridge cases, the computer plug, the

papers that had been thrown all over the office. He explained how he had established that the shooting had come before the emptying of the file cabinets.

In cross-examination, Stott asked if anything had been found at the crime scene that established Afton's presence that night.

"No," Officer Durning said.

Had any fingerprints been found?

Officer Durning said they had found some of Afton's fingerprints, but that this was hardly unusual since Afton and Sloane worked together. He admitted that no prints of Afton's had been found on the filing cabinet or the computer plug.

"Did you find any fingerprints on the murder weapon?" Stott asked.

"No."

Witness: the firearms examiner

Firearms examiner Peter Westcott testified next. He explained how he had concluded that the bullet found in the deceased and the bullet found in the deceased's office had both come from the gun that had been recovered from the water close to James Afton's building. Stott had no questions.

Witness: the forensic biologist

The forensic biologist testified that the DNA profile from the blood on Afton's jacket matched the DNA profile of Edwin Sloane.

Stott had spoken to the biologist during his trial preparations. He had also had the jacket examined by his own experts and had spoken to them about the significance of their findings. In his cross-examination, he asked if there was any way to tell how long the blood had been on the jacket. The biologist said that there wasn't, but that one could expect blood to flake off a leather jacket eventually.

"All of it?" Stott asked.

"There's no way of knowing," the biologist said. "It depends on how often the jacket was worn and under what circumstances."

"So there's no way to say for sure how long the blood had been on Mr. Afton's jacket?"

"No."

Witness: the forensic chemist

The forensic chemist was called. He explained what gunshot residue was and said that it had been found on the sleeve of Afton's jacket. He said that while this didn't prove that Afton had fired the gun, it did show that he had been close by when a gun was fired or, at least, that the sleeve had been in contact with a surface on which there was gunshot residue.

In cross-examination, Stott drew on what he had learned from his experts. He asked the chemist if he could say how long the gunshot residue had been there.

"No," the chemist said. "But one would expect gunshot residue to flake off eventually."

Stott asked how long that would take.

"It could take days," the chemist said. "It depends on what happened to the jacket — whether it had been worn much or washed or sent to the dry cleaner."

"If the jacket hadn't been worn or cleaned, could it take a week?" Stott asked.

"It's possible," the chemist said.

"Two weeks or even longer?"

The chemist said he didn't know, but he thought it was unlikely.

"But is it possible?" Stott said.

"Yes," the chemist said. "It's possible."

Then he asked if the chemist could tell whether the gunshot residue came from a specific firearm.

"No," the chemist said. "There's no way to do that."

• • •

"Correct me if I'm wrong," I said, "but it sounds as if the defence was scoring points."

Uncle Joe didn't correct me.

"So what happened?" I asked.

Proving Guilt

To prove someone guilty, the Crown must demonstrate several things.

That an offense was committed. This is called the *actus reus*. For example, Mr. Pink fires a gun and kills Mr. Green.

That the offense was intended. This is called the *mens rea*. This involves understanding the state of mind of the accused. For example, when Mr. Pink fired his gun, did he do it on purpose or was it an accident? If he did it on purpose, did he intend to kill Mr. Green or was he trying to frighten or warn him? If the charge is first-degree murder, the prosecution must also show that the act was planned and deliberate.

The identity of the guilty party. Was it really Mr. Pink who killed Mr. Green?

The place, time and date that the offence occurred — although a crime can be proved without the last two.

CHAPTER 16

The Defence Case

"NEXT, THE DEFENCE presented its case," Uncle Joe said.

"And?"

• • •

There was no proof that Afton had been in the Belmont Building that night. In fact, no one could say exactly who had or hadn't been there. If Afton had gassed up at 10:45 PM and then gone straight home, he would have arrived there at eleven, as he had told police. Valerie Murphy couldn't dispute this with certainty. And while Afton may have had a financial reason for killing Sloane, other people with a similar motive hadn't resorted to violence. Besides, there was nothing to show that he had known about Sloane's plans. There was no physical evidence tying Afton to either the murder scene or the murder weapon.

It was possible to argue that the Crown had not proved its case beyond a reasonable doubt. The big problem for the defence was the jacket.

A person accused of a crime cannot be forced to testify. In many cases, the person does not. But Stott had been watching the jury. He was pretty sure that they understood some of the weaknesses in the Crown's case. But he was also pretty sure that they had serious doubts. For example, how had the gun come to be found at exactly the spot where Valerie Murphy had seen Afton throw something into the water? Why did Afton have gunshot residue on his jacket? How had Sloane's blood got on Afton's jacket? Those were questions the jury would want answers to.

It was always risky to put the defendant on the stand. If he testified, the Crown could cross-examine. Maybe Afton would get flustered. Maybe he wouldn't express himself well.

Stott thought it over carefully. He decided it would be riskier for Afton to remain silent. He would have to tell his story to the jury, just as he had told it to Stott.

Afton agreed. He said he wanted to tell the truth. He said he wasn't afraid of Wesolowski.

But before Stott called Afton, he called two other witnesses.

Witness: Dylan Dumont

Stott called Dylan Dumont. He asked Dylan to explain why he had come to town. He asked about his relationship with Sloane. Dylan admitted that he resented his father and that he had been angry that his father hadn't offered to pay for his education. He also admitted that he had told his father, that night, that he hated him and never wanted to see him again.

"How did your father react to that?"

"He didn't seem to care."

"How did that make you feel?"

"Angry."

Stott asked more questions. Dylan admitted that he didn't have an alibi for the night of the murder. He said he had been at the Belmont Building the day before. He admitted to having known about his father's gun and about the will. His mother had told him a long time ago.

"You told the police you didn't know about the will."

"Yes."

"You lied to the police, didn't you?"

"What I meant was, I didn't know how much he was leaving me," Dylan said.

"In fact, how much did your father leave you?" Stott asked.

"One million dollars."

Witness: Martha Cooper

Martha Cooper wasn't happy to be called by the defence, but she answered Stott's questions. Yes, she said, it was true that Mr. Sloane had suffered from nosebleeds. He'd had them often. When he'd had them, he had bled a lot. It was also true that on at least one occasion, he had bled so much that when she tried to help him, some of his blood had spilled on her dress.

Witness: James Afton

The defence called James Afton. Afton swore to tell the truth. Stott knew how Afton would answer his questions — he had heard Afton's version of events in detail.

Afton explained that he and the victim had been friends for decades. He told the court how he had encouraged Sloane to write children's books. He explained how he had helped turn Sloane the author into Scarr Enterprises. He explained the plans for the new TV series and said that Sloane had been excited about them. He said that shortly before the murder, Sloane was supposed to have met with Andrew Mackie, but instead started stalling and wouldn't say why. Afton said he was surprised to learn, after Sloane's death, that Sloane had planned to cancel the deal.

Then Stott asked about the events of that night. Afton told the court the same story he had told Stott many months before. He said that after he left the book launch, he took a walk to clear his head. The bookstore had been noisy and he'd been worried about the meeting with Mackie. When his headache faded, he got in his car to go home. He noticed that he was low on gas, so he drove to the gas station he often went to. It was close to the Belmont Building, but he didn't go into the building. He drove straight from the gas station to his condo. He wasn't sure of the exact time that he arrived home, but he was pretty sure it was around eleven o'clock. He parked his car and headed across to the waterfront. He often took long walks along the water, late at night. It calmed him down. He skipped stones on the water, as he often did. That was probably what his neighbour saw. He did not throw a gun into the water.

Then Stott zeroed in on the jacket. To him, it was critical to the case. The jury would want to know how gunshot residue and the victim's blood happened to be on Afton's jacket.

Afton said he wore the jacket to the book launch, but got warm and took it off when he got to his car. He left it in the car overnight and then wore it to the office the next day, where he hung it in his closet. He said that at first he'd been surprised to learn there was blood on it. He supposed it could have got there a few weeks before the murder when Sloane had had a particularly bad nosebleed. He'd had them all the time — ever since he was a kid. Afton said that once he had got blood on his pants from one of Sloane's famous nosebleeds.

"What about the gunshot residue?" Stott asked.

Here Afton hung his head. He said he told the police he hadn't seen Sloane's gun in a long time. This wasn't quite true, he admitted.

About six weeks before the murder, he and Sloane drove up north to Andrew Mackie's cottage to talk about the TV deal. They stopped on the side of the road for a break and Sloane took out the gun. Afton hated that gun. Sloane didn't have a permit for it. And Sloane acted strangely sometimes. Everyone thought of him as Mr. Nice Kid's Author. But he had a dark side. When he brought out the gun, Afton felt uneasy. Sloane wanted to know if Afton had ever fired a gun before. Afton said he hadn't. Sloane pressed him to give it a try. Afton resisted. But Sloane pestered him. Finally, to satisfy him, Afton fired it. Maybe that's why there was gunshot residue on his jacket. Unfortunately, no one else was around at the time. He wasn't even sure exactly where they were — somewhere between Barrie and Orillia. He didn't tell anyone about the incident.

Stott asked why he hadn't told the police the truth about the gun. Afton said he was afraid he would become a suspect.

"What happened to the other clothes you were wearing that night?" Stott asked.

"I sent them to the cleaners."

"But you didn't send the jacket to the cleaners."

"No," Afton said. "Why would I?"

Uncle Joe leaned over to the Crown. He had been at the Crown's table for the whole trial, watching the jury and listening to what all the witnesses said. Now he whispered something into Wesolowski's ear. Wesolowski whispered something back. Uncle Joe got up and left the courtroom.

Uncle Joe and his partner contacted Valerie Murphy, who said she was sure Afton's black leather jacket was new only a couple of weeks before the murder. He had bought it from a store in Yorkville. If she was right about when he had bought the jacket, then Afton couldn't have been wearing it in mid-March when he claimed to have fired Sloane's gun. The detectives decided to check.

There were several stores in the Yorkville area that sold men's leather jackets, but only two sold jackets as expensive as Afton's. The detectives asked both stores to check their records. Sure enough, Afton had bought his jacket at the second store in early April, less than three weeks before the murder.

Wesolowski had started her cross-examination of James Afton. She asked him how the murder weapon had ended up where it had.

"I don't know," Afton said.

"It's a remarkable coincidence, isn't it?" Wesolowski said.

Afton agreed that it was.

When she saw the two detectives, Wesolowski asked for a brief recess. After she had studied the receipt, she had to disclose its existence to Stott. But Stott couldn't discuss it with his client. Defence is not allowed to talk to an accused during cross-examination.

When the trial resumed, Wesolowski asked, "Isn't it true that you lied to the police about when you had last seen Mr. Sloane's gun?"

"Yes, it's true," Afton said. He looked contrite.

"Did you tell the truth when you said you had fired the gun nearly six weeks before the murder and that the gunshot residue must have got on your jacket at that time?"

"Yes, that's the truth," Afton said.

Wesolowski asked Afton how many black leather jackets he owned.

"Just one."

"Was it the black leather jacket that we saw earlier — the one with the label in it from a store in Yorkville?"

"Yes."

Wesolowski produced the store receipt for the jacket and entered it as evidence. She showed it to Afton and asked him if he knew what it was.

"A receipt."

"From what store?"

He read out the name of the store.

"What did you buy at that store?"

"A black leather jacket."

Wesolowski asked him to read out the date on the receipt.

When he did, the courtroom was silent.

"Can you explain, Mr. Afton, how you got gunshot residue on the sleeve of a jacket three weeks before you even owned it?"

Afton could not.

Stott had a chance to redirect — to ask further questions so as to clarify what Afton had said. His mission was to offer an alternative way that the gunshot residue and blood could have got on the jacket. He asked what Afton had done with the jacket, the day after Scarr was shot.

"I wore it to the office and hung it in the closet." He said he had left it there.

"Do you ever lock your office?" Stott asked.

"No."

"So anyone could go in and out?"

"That's right."

"Do you know if your jacket was in the closet from the time you hung it there, the morning after the murder, until the time the police seized it?"

"I don't know," Afton said. "I didn't check on it or anything."

"Is it possible someone could have removed the jacket for any period of time?"

"Yes," Afton said.

• • •

"You nailed him!" I said. "I knew it!"

"Most cases don't have such dramatic endings," Uncle Joe said. "But, yeah, we thought we had him pretty good."

"Did he confess?"

"No, he didn't."

• • •

Closing arguments in a real court aren't as brief as they appear on television. In long, serious cases, Crown attorneys and defence lawyers may talk for two hours or more in their closing statements to the jury. It can take that long to go over all of the evidence and show what it proves — or fails to prove.

If the defence presents no evidence at trial, the Crown closes first. In this case, though, the defence went first.

Stott pointed out the weaknesses in the Crown's case. No one had seen Afton at the Belmont Building, and there was no physical evidence proving he had been there or handled the murder weapon. There was no proof that he wasn't home at eleven o'clock as he had said. He reminded the jury that others had a financial motive to kill Sloane. Then he reviewed the forensic evidence and reminded the jury what it did not prove. It did not prove that the blood on Afton's jacket had got there the night of the murder. It only proved that it was Sloane's blood.

The jury had heard Martha Cooper say that Sloane had often had nosebleeds. She had also testified that blood from these nosebleeds had got on her dress at least once before. The same thing had happened to James Afton. He reminded the jury that there was no way of telling how long the gunshot residue had been on Afton's jacket or what gun had deposited it there. He pointed out that the jacket had been hanging in a place where anyone could get at it. Someone who wanted to put blame on Afton could have taken the jacket and fired a gun, any gun, which would have left gunshot residue on the sleeve.

Wesolowski had the final word. She went through her case step by step. She reminded the jury of Afton's motive and the fact that he had no alibi. She focused on the discovery of the gun and on the jacket. Surely it was too much of a coincidence that he was seen throwing something into the water the night of the murder and that the police had then found the gun at that very spot. She reminded the jury that Afton had lied to the police about when he had last seen the gun. He had lied again when he told the court how gunshot residue had got onto his jacket.

There were just too many lies and coincidences, she said, all designed to conceal the truth. And the truth was that James Afton had murdered Edwin Sloane for financial gain.

CHAPTER 17
Guilty or Not Guilty?

"AND?" I said. "What happened?"

"The judge gave his charge to the jury. He reviewed the evidence for them, and explained the law and their duties. Then the jury went out to deliberate," Uncle Joe said.

"What did you do?"

"The Crown has a trial room at the courthouse. We hung out there. At first when a jury goes out, you know they're going to be out for a while. You expect to wait. But after they've been out for a while, you start to wonder if they're still out because they're arguing about something. If they are, are they arguing that he's innocent or that he's guilty? Sometimes the jury has questions. If they do, they have to write down the question for the judge. Then the judge calls in both lawyers and they all talk about how to answer the question. Sometimes the jury's questions can give you a clue about what they're thinking."

"Did the jury have any questions in this case?"

Uncle Joe shook his head. "They weren't out for very long, either. Less than two hours."

"Is that good or bad?"

"You're never sure," Uncle Joe said. "Sometimes you think when they decide so fast, it's because they're sure the guy is guilty. Sometimes you think it's the opposite.

When we got the call that they had reached a verdict, we went back to the courtroom. The judge came in first. The courtroom was packed. You know how it is at a wedding — one side of the church is filled with the bride's friends and family, the other side with the groom's? Well, it was almost like that. One side of the courtroom was filled with the deceased's family and relatives. The other side was filled with people who supported the accused. The media was there. Then the jury came in. And you can't help it — when they come in, you try to read them. A lot of people say that if they look at the accused, that means they're going to acquit him and if they don't look at him, they're going to convict. More often than not that's true. But not always."

"What about in this case?"

"In this case, they didn't look at him."

"What did they say?"

"Guilty. They found James Afton guilty of the murder of Edwin Sloane. The defence polled the jury — asked each juror one by one to say if they agreed with the verdict."

"Why? They already said guilty."

Uncle Joe shrugged. "It's their last shot. If one juror says no, then a mistrial is declared. But I can't think of even one case where that's ever happened."

"You must have been jumping for joy, Uncle Joe. You did it. You nailed the guy."

Uncle Joe shook his head.

"Nobody wins in murder cases," he said. "Everybody loses. It's just a matter of how much. The deceased's friends and family can take comfort when someone is convicted, but their loved one is still gone. It's just as

tough on the accused's family. Most accused have loved ones who are decent people and who are devastated that he's going away for the rest of his life for what he did. So at the end of the day, even though you did your job and you did it well, it's a tragedy."

Just then I heard a strange noise. It sounded like a big truck, or a —

"Snow plow!" said Uncle Joe. "Finally!"

Notes

1. James N. Gilbert, *Criminal Investigation*, second edition (Charles E. Merrill Publishing Company, 1986)
2. Technical Working Group on Crime Scene Investigation, *Crime Scene Investigation: A Guide for Law Enforcement* (National Institute of Justice, U.S. Department of Justice, 2000)
3. *Report on the Law of Coroners* (Ontario Law Reform Commission, 1995)
4. Joseph P. LaDurantey and Daniel R. Sullivan, *Criminal Investigation Standards* (Harper & Row Publishers, 1980)
5. M/Sgt. Hayden B. Baldwin, Retired, "Basic Equipment for Crime Scene Investigators" [Internet article, cited 2000]. Available at www.feinc.net/equipmt.htm
6. National Medicolegal Review Panel, *Death Investigation: A Guide for the Scene Investigator* (National Institute of Justice, U.S. Department of Justice, 1999)
7. *NRA Firearms Fact Book*, second edition (National Rifle Association of America, 1988)
8. "DNA: Deoxyribonucleic acid" (Centre of Forensic Sciences, 1999)
9. Legal Line (Legal Information Ontario) [Internet database, cited 2000]. Available at www.LegalLine.ca
10. Neil Boyd, *Canadian Law: An Introduction* (Harcourt Brace & Company Canada, 1995)
11. Don Stuart and Ronald Joseph Delisle, *Learning Canadian Criminal Law*, sixth edition (Carswell, 1997)

Index

Actus reus 150
Affidavit 121
Ammunition (as evidence) 27, 38–39, 43–44, 58–59, 64, 79–80, 85, 87–89, 104–105
Arrest warrant 112–113
Autopsy 24, 59–64
Autopsy diagram *62*
Bail 114, 119–122
Blood (as evidence) 40–41, 42, 63, 83, 84, 89–90, 92, 93–94, 103, 111
Body (as evidence) 14, 24–26, 43, 91. *See also* Postmortem examination
Bullet. *See* Ammunition
Bunny suit. *See* Contamination suit
Canadian Charter of Rights and Freedoms 114, 133
Canvass 78, 97, 113
Cartridge case. *See* Ammunition; Firearms and toolmarks examination
Circumstantial evidence 112, 114–115, 118, 122, 138
Closing arguments 159–161
Clothing (as evidence) 60, 61, 63, 84, 89, 107, 109, 148–150
Contamination suit 17, 34
Contusion ring 63
Coroner, medical examiner 14, 23, 24–26, 28–30
Crime lab 58–59, 60, 66, 82–92, 94. *See also* Forensic scientists
Crime scene investigation. *See* Forensic Identification
Crime-scene sketch 26, *36*, 146
Criminal defence lawyer 111–112, 116–117, 118, 120, 131–132. *See also* Jury; Preliminary inquiry; Pre-trial conference; Trial
  Preparations for trial 125, 126–127
Cross-examination. *See* Examination and cross-examination
Crown attorney 117–119, 120, 121, 126, 150–151. *See also* Jury; Preliminary inquiry; Pre-trial conference; Trial
  Preparations for trial 123–125, 138–139
Direct evidence 114
DNA analysis 40–41, 83, 89–90, 93–94, 95, 111, 121, 148
Evidence, documentary, handling
  Crime-scene sketches 26, *36*, 148
  Notes 12–15, 16, 19, 30–31, 34, 39, 40, 42, 53, 55, 61–62, 79, 125, 126
  Photographs 39–40, 42, 60, 62, 79, 83, 106, 146
  Videotape 39, 74, 78, 113, 143
  Witness statements 65, 96–97, 118, 121, 126
Evidence, oral, collecting
  Examination and cross-examination 131, 138–150. *See also* Trial

Questioning, interviewing 12–13, 15, 21–23, 49–57, 65, 66–79, 112, 117, 124–126
Evidence, physical, handling 33, 84
Ammunition 27, 38–39, 43–44, 58–59, 64, 79–80, 85, 87–89, 104–105
Blood 40–41, 42, 63, 83, 84, 89–90, 92, 93–94, 103, 111
Body 14, 24–26, 43, 91. *See also* Postmortem examination
Clothing 60, 61, 63, 84, 89, 107, 109, 148–150
Fingerprints 41, *42*, 42–43, 60, 84, 103
Footprints 35, 38, 41, 43
Footwear impressions 35, 43
Murder weapon 103–105, 148
Trace evidence (hairs and fibres) 38, 41, *42*, 63, 83, 84, 89
Evidence, types
Circumstantial 112, 114–115, 118, 122, 138
Direct 114
Examination and cross-examination 131, 138–150. *See also* Trial
Examination-in-chief 138
Expert witness 137
Fibres. *See* Trace evidence
Fingerprints (as evidence) 41, *42*, 42–43, 60, 84, 103
Firearms and toolmarks examiner, examination 27–28, 58–59, 60, 63–64, 83, 85–89, 103–105, 148
Firearms discharge residue 61, 103–104
First-degree murder 91, 132, 150
First responding officer 11–19
Responsibilities 16-19
Footprints 35, 38, 41, 43
Footwear impressions 35, 43
Forensic biologist 83, 89–90, 103, 110–111, 148–149
Forensic chemist 83, 109–110, 149–150
Forensic Identification 14, 23, 24, 26, 27–28, 33–44, 59–60, 66, 70, 146–148
Equipment 45–47
Forensic pathologist 24, 59–64
Forensic photoanalyst 83
Forensic scientists 82–83, 124, 137
Biologist 83, 89–90, 103, 110–111, 148–149
Chemist 83, 109–110, 149–150
Firearms and toolmarks examiner 27, 58–59, 60, 63–64, 83, 85–89, 103–105, 148
Pathologist 24, 59–64
Photoanalyst 83
Toxicologist 83, 91–92
Forensic toxicologist 83, 91–92
Gun. *See* Murder weapon; Firearms and toolmarks examination
Gunshot residue 110, 121, 149–150, 155–156, 158, 160
Hairs. *See* Trace evidence
"Hearsay" evidence 136–137
Ident. *See* Forensic Identification

Interviewing. *See* Questioning, interviewing
Jury. *See also* Trial
Deliberation 162–163
Delivering verdict 163
Selection 133–134
Lands and grooves 87, 88
Locard's Theory (Edmond Locard) 33, 84
Medical examiner. *See* Coroner, medical examiner
Mens rea 150
Murder weapon (as evidence) 103–105, 148
Note-taking 12–15, 16, 19, 30–31, 34, 39, 40, 42, 53, 55, 61–62, 79, 125, 126
Oath 136
Opening statement 135–136
Perjury 136
Photographs (as evidence) 39–40, 42, 60, 62, 79, 83, 106, 146
Postmortem examination 24, 59–64
Postmortem lividity 25
Pre-trial conference 131–132
Preliminary inquiry 123, 128–129, 138–139
Questioning, interviewing 12–13, 15, 21–23, 49–57, 65, 66–79, 112, 117, 124–126
Reasonable doubt 118, 133, 139, 153
Rifling 87, 88
Rights 111, 114, 132
Rigor mortis 25
Search warrant 107, 112, 132
Second-degree murder 91, 132
Surety 120–122
Testimony. *See* Witness statements; Examination and cross-examination
Trace evidence (hairs and fibres) 38, 41, *42*, 63, 83, 84, 89
Transfer stain 35–36
Trial 15, 91, 114, 117, 134–163. *See also* Pre-trial conference; Preliminary inquiry
Videotape (as evidence) 39, 74, 78, 113, 143
Water recovery tank *104*, 105
Witnesses 136–137. *See also* Canvass, Criminal defence lawyer; Crown attorney; Direct evidence; Questioning; Witness statements
Witness statements 65, 96–97, 118, 121, 126
Wounds 25, 29, 41, 60. *See also* Postmortem examination